The Hillingdon Fox

PET

Jan Mark

The Hillingdon Fox

TURTON & CHAMBERS

For Alan Payne

© Jan Mark 1991
First published in
England and Australia 1991
by Turton & Chambers Ltd
Station Road, Woodchester
Stroud, Glos GL5 5EQ, England
and 10 Armagh Street
Victoria Park, Perth
Western Australia 6100

Typesetting by Avonset
Midsomer Norton, Bath
Printed in England by
Short Run Press, Exeter

CIP Data available
from the British Library

ISBN 1 872148 60 3

The Hillingdon Fox

Thursday 16.8.90

I never kept a diary before. I'm not at all sure that I want to keep one now, but time passes and something tells me that I'll be sorry if I don't. In 1937 three men set up an organization called Mass Observation, which was thousands of people all over the country writing down day-to-day things as they happened, as a kind of national diary of what it was like to be alive at the time. Politicians keep diaries and think that they matter, and publish them. I've read one of those, well, tried to. He was a Labour MP so I suppose he thought he was a man of the people, but he might have been living on another planet. There were no people like me in it, for example.

It's my seventeenth birthday. About a month ago I began to think about this diary, about keeping it, that is. And I've been putting it off, ever since. I was embarrassed just thinking about it, and I'm embarrassed now. It seems so pretentious, sitting alone in an empty room, writing something down that no one will ever read, because this isn't going to be Mass Observation, no way. This is going to be innermost thoughts. Writing down innermost thoughts is so egotistical – no, *egoistical*. I always get those two words mixed up. So do most people, judging by what gets written in the papers. And I'm not going to cross anything out. I nearly put a line through egotistical, but you can't cross out what you think, so there it stays.

Last week, Saturday, I bought this book, 200 pages narrow feint with margins and two little holes for filing. It could have been for school, that's what I've been telling myself ever since, but I thought, when I bought it, if I do use it as a diary I'll begin it on my birthday. That's why I'm here now. It's taken me about twenty minutes even to get this far but I must admit that already it's getting easier. It still seems pretentious, in a way, believing that what I think matters enough to go down on paper, in fact to start with it was like talking aloud and being sure that someone was listening.

I've got to keep me out of this. I'm not meant to be in it anyway – this is not going to be *about* me – but I thought, after sitting up here in the bedroom for *two hours*, that the only way to get started was to put down anything that came into my head. Well, now we know what's been in and out of my head, let's get down to business.

There is an ancient Chinese curse that goes something like, 'May it be your misfortune to live in interesting times'. It seems to me I've always lived in interesting times: Thatcherism, mass unemployment, high interest rates, rocketing mortgages, inflation, AIDS, the Rushdie affair, the Bomb. Last Christmas it looked as if we could all stop worrying and forget the Bomb, in fact one of the reasons I'm starting this diary is because I wish I'd been keeping it last year when the Berlin Wall came down and Poland and Czecho-slovakia booted out the Communists, and the Ceausescus were shot.

Now we can all *start* worrying again. On 2 August Saddam Hussein, the President of Iraq, invaded Kuwait. Thank God he didn't do it a couple of years ago, Mum said, or Reagan would have nuked Baghdad in his sleep, but the word is Crisis, all the same.

Today King Hussein of Jordan was having talks with President Bush and then on the radio – not ours, I heard it from next-door's garden – they said that all foreigners, British and American, in Kuwait and Iraq, must report to a particular hotel. *All* of them, about six thousand, and four thousand of them are British. It looks like internment, they said on the news at 5.40.

I'm already beginning to wish I'd started to write all this when I first thought of it, last month. Then I'd have had a complete record of the conflict. I could do a quick run-down tomorrow, but it doesn't matter all that much. No one else is going to read it. It's *annoying*, that's all, starting in the middle of something. Still, that's life, isn't it? You always come in in the middle. I was born in 1973. I must find out what I arrived in the middle of.

Dinner time. I promised to be in tonight for a special birthday nosh. I smelled fish, earlier. Calamaris, with luck.

APRIL 2ND 1982 FRIDAY

Greetings to the Twenty-First Century!

Let me introduce myself. My name is Gerald Marshall and I am eighteen years old, having been born on January 17th 1964. I live at 8, Grosvenor Avenue, Calderley, Oxon, with my parents Anthony and Elizabeth Marshall, and my brothers, Geoffrey and Hugh. Geoffrey was born on February 3rd 1972 and Hugh on August 16th 1973. At the moment I am one of 730 pupils at Calderley Comprehensive School although I shall be leaving this summer to spend a year working on a kibbutz (a collective farm in Israel) and after that I shall go to the University of East Anglia to read for a degree in physics.

The Time Capsule which you have just opened contains as true a picture as we can contrive of the state of the nation. The sculpture beneath which it has been buried will be erected on May 5th 1982. As chairman of the committee I have taken it upon myself to keep a diary of the month between now and the evening of May 3rd when we shall seal the capsule and place it beneath the site of the sculpture, to give an accurate account of life in this English town for those who come after us.

It is our intent that the capsule will remain concealed for exactly one hundred years. We have a saying in the late twentieth century: 'It will all be the same in a hundred years.' At this naivety you will probably be smiling, being in a position to know that many things are *not* the same, but whatever changes time has wrought since I write this will be immaterial to us, confident as we are that the chances of any of us living to be one hundred and eighteen are remote to say the least! It is quite possible that none of us will live even to be nineteen. This then is our immortality, as you grow to know us over the next month. We are: Robert Whiting, Naseem Amin, Lucy Ashton, Jo-Ann Rugg, Timothy Finch, Jon Lo, William Sargent, William Thomson, Mark Lovell and myself, Gerald Marshall. I shall make no observations upon the events of today, beyond the fact that it is the last day of the Easter term. After school we, the committee, met in the sixth-form common room and laid plans for the contents of the capsule. (Perhaps you have seen them already. We as yet do not even know what they will be.) However, the observations which will interest you must be on world events. The Northern Irish Secretary, James Prior, in this the thirteenth year of the Troubles, has produced new plans to devolve power in Ulster, and two soldiers have died in an IRA ambush.

Two Polish military pilots have escaped to the West with their families. A happy ending in Poland looks as unlikely as a happy ending in Ulster, but Lech Walesa's wife says that she thinks her husband is confident that the Martial Law authorities will 'resume dialogue' with him.

In the Gulf War between Iran and Iraq the Iraqi President, Saddam Hussein, has suffered an over-whelming defeat. An Iranian spokesman says that the Iraqi army is broken as a fighting force and it can only be a matter of time before it is driven from Iranian territory. It is only a couple of years ago, but I have to confess that already I have forgotten how this conflict started.

Yesterday the Royal Navy sent the destroyer *Exeter*

to the Falkland Islands in the South Atlantic, and it does look as if the Falklands themselves will be invaded. As you probably know, this all began when Argentinian scrap metal merchants raised the Argentine flag on the island of South Georgia. I can imagine you reading about this in history books – if such things still exist – as the 'Scrap Metal War', rather like 'The War of Jenkins' Ear'. Out of the ten members of the committee only one knew that South Georgia existed and all but two thought the Falklands were off the coast of Scotland.

Remember, our watchword is: It will all be the same in a hundred years!

Friday 17.8.90

A search for a way back from the brink – is what they said on the News last night, after dinner. It *was* calamaris, by the way, with a samphire salad.

When I went to bed I was wondering what I'd be writing about tonight, whether that great international muddle of troops and tanks and planes and missiles would have rolled over the Saudi border, but what happened was nothing at all. The British and American residents turned up at the hotels with all the food they had at home (that *was* sinister, as President Bush said) but no one was expecting them and so they all went home again.

That strikes me as funny, but this time tomorrow it may turn out not to be funny at all. And it couldn't have been funny for them. I think I meant ludicrous. At any rate, at the moment there seems to have been more slaughter on the home front. On Tuesday two Tornado jets collided over the Humber estuary and on Thursday *two more* did the same – near Hull, I think it was. The Ministry of Defence says there is no link and perhaps there isn't, apart from jointly wiping out several billions of pounds' worth of aeroplane and killing five men.

And employment's up again, inflation's up again. At least we've had some rain. (Droughts, climatic change, global warming, the depletion of the ozone layer, the Greenhouse Effect: just a few of the interesting things I left out yesterday.) The Gulf Crisis has knocked everything else off the front pages. At the end of July there was an insurrection in Trinidad, six hundred civilians massacred in Liberia, a member of our parliament was killed by the IRA. Now, suddenly, nothing but Iraq. I can remember when there was nothing but Eastern Europe, and before that, it didn't matter what happened, the USSR always grabbed the headlines. Ah, the dear dead days of the Cold War. This one may not be a war yet, but it's hot. The Falklands weren't a war either, until we started winning. I didn't notice that at the time, I was only nine, but it struck me afterwards. Gerald was full of it, Mum used to get really embarrassed when he started up in front of visitors. He was very right-wing in those days. He used to say 'This country needs a war,' though he never said why, and when it came he wasn't in it. I don't know what he's like now. I haven't really seen all that much of him since he left school, in '82, same year as the Falklands. He left home at the same time. Now he works on some nuclear energy project in Geneva and he'll be getting married later this year, to a Swiss. I expect he'll settle there for good.

The other big news story yesterday was A-level results, big news because the people who sat it this year are the first ones to come on from GCSE instead of O-level. The examiners say the pass rate's up, the right-wing politicos say that's because the standards are down. It's all politics, see? No other way does anything educational hit the headlines. Geoff got three As, the brilliant git. He didn't even work very hard. Perhaps standards *are* falling – Gerry only got two Bs and a C and he worked his butt off, or said he did.

My turn next year. No doubt the pass rate will drop dramatically and me with it. Just think, this time next year I shall be sitting here – possibly – recording my grades for posterity.

I don't know why I wrote that. This is not for posterity. If I thought anyone was going to read it I wouldn't be writing it, or if I were, I'd be writing it better than this; long elegant compound sentences like I do for Eng. Lit.

If Geoff can get an A for Eng. Lit. I'm damn sure I can. There's eight years between Gerry and Geoff but only eighteen months between Geoff and me. I think I was a mistake, to tell you the truth. In spite of all precautions, a determined sperm got through!

Gerry didn't send me a birthday present. He didn't even send me a card, the unnatural swine. Right, I'll send him one instead. I'll get it tomorrow, a pretty thing with ribbons and flowers. I wonder if you can get cards that say 'Thank you for forgetting my birthday'?

I was going to write to him anyway, on account of some news that

APRIL 3RD 1982 SATURDAY

First of all, the International Situation: yesterday the Argentinians invaded the Falklands and the Cabinet is in emergency session. Diplomatic relations have been broken off and all army units were recalled last night. Lord Carrington, our Foreign Secretary, will not say if we are actually at war. The Falklands are seven thousand miles away. The nuclear submarine *Superb* is already on the way, but to fight the invasion a full-scale task force will be needed. The United States has called for immediate withdrawal of Argentine forces but at the UN the Soviets and non-aligned delegates refuse to vote without instructions from their governments. This is a typical reaction, of course, to anything that America does!

The invaders claim that the islands have surrendered but the reports of this seem to have come from a radio 'ham' who says there was a three-hour battle. Air Commodore Frow, of the Falklands Office in London, says there should be 'graduated military response' including the H Bomb if necessary. This provoked considerable disagreement at home. My mother remarked that if we dropped an H Bomb on the Falklands the Argentinians would be welcome to what was left. She is of the opinion that our presence in the Falklands is ludicrous anyway, rather like Argentina maintaining sovereignty of the Channel Islands. My father said that General Galtieri (the Argentine President) must be stopped and that it was an act of the utmost cynicism to wage war solely to revive public support for an unpopular right-wing administration with rocketing inflation. My mother said, 'Quite. I should have expected better from a British government,' which I felt, to be honest, was deplorably flippant.

In the USSR Leonid Brezhnev's health is worsening and it is possible that he has had a stroke. My mother said that he could have been clinically dead for years and no one would have noticed; look at Reagan. I recount these rather trivial exchanges so that you may see what a gulf of opinion can exist in one household!

Chelsea Football Club has been sold. Is (Association) football still our national game, I wonder, in 2082?

Here in Calderley the focus of interest is the closure of Restmore the furniture-makers, which will result in the loss of 117 jobs. This must be typical of events in many small towns in the United Kingdom, as inefficient, antiquated firms with unreliable machinery find themselves unable to compete in a monetarist society. The demise of Restmore is the inevitable result of overmanning and underproduction. Had it closed when it should have done, in 1978, those who have lost their jobs would already have found alternative employment. I must say I envy you the perspective of history, to be able to look back at this month in our lives, this microcosm of the nation as a whole.

This morning, Will Sargent, Lucy Ashton and I went to see the Headmaster and were shown the sculpture, in a photograph, beneath which this diary and the Time Capsule will be buried. There is no need to describe it to you as you will have long been familiar with it. It will have been a part of your lives as it will become a part of ours, although not for very long in our case, as we stand on the threshold of maturity and prepare to disperse into adulthood.

A year ago the school was given a sum of money by a foundation, to erect a piece of sculpture on the campus, and young artists (under twenty-five) were invited to submit designs. We were all allowed to vote and the winning design was commissioned. As far as I can tell from the photograph it has changed considerably since we saw the original sketches and it is difficult to imagine its actual size and appearance: eight feet high in Bath stone. I can tell you, though, that it appears to be a mellow golden colour and I would hazard a guess that by the time you read this, age and pollution will have rendered it otherwise. The sculptor, Siobhan McInnes, is, as I write, totally unknown, having left art school only last year. Now I wonder, has she become one of the great names of twentieth-century art, or is she still totally unknown? I wish you could tell me. It is impossible these days to guess whether or not an artist will be famous, let alone whether or not he is any good!

Afterwards, Will, Lucy and I met up with Jon Lo and we walked into town together. The committee appointed to oversee the Time Capsule is all drawn from our second-year sixth, but we four are close friends and will probably form the nucleus of decision-making. Today we each drew up a list of things that we thought might go into the capsule. Initially someone had suggested newspapers but lack of space precluded that – hence this diary as a substitute. We may put in one or two so that you can see what our local and national press was like in 1982. (You know whether or not we did!) We are agreed though that we should include photographs and perhaps video and audio tapes. We do hope that you still have the means to play them.

You may be wondering what we have used for the capsule itself. It is in fact one of the containers in which the Education Committee sends out films. The black plastic shroud, which (probably) surrounds it as an additional precaution against the infiltration of moisture, is known as a 'bin-liner', a means of disposing of household waste and normally collected by 'dustmen' every week.

Saturday 18.8.90

As I was saying when I was so rudely interrupted – by Geoff, wanting to go and paint the town red on account of his A-levels. He said his celebration got delayed by my birthday thrash.

As I was saying when I so rudely interrupted myself, I was intending to write to Gerry anyway, because I've got news for him that will get right up his tiny nose. Me and my peer group (sounds good, that) will be the last sixth form but one. Because of falling rolls (raining baps and cobs, ho ho) we are going to amalgamate with the Mercery Lane School and stop at the fifth year. Mercery Lane will become a sixth form college. But we are too small to contain all the Mercery Lane mob so a new fifth form block is going to be built in the corner of the quadrangle – well, mainly all over the quadrangle. It must have been on the cards for ages but we only heard at the end of last term.

Now, at the corner of the quadrangle is The Feelie. This is a nasty stone *thing* on a plinth, over two metres high – nearly three with the plinth – that looks as if it was carved out of very old cheese. I think it has an official name, something like 'Untitled, 1982', but for years it's been known as The Feelie because if it looks like anything at all it is a huge groping hand. Give us our due, no one has scrawled any graffiti on it, but people leave Coke cans standing on the plinth and there is usually a traffic cone perched on top.

The Feelie went up the year Gerry left school and as far as I can remember, he had something to do with its being there. I think the sixth form were allowed to vote on a set of submitted designs – they had a democratic head in those days, not like the current Fascist lackey H. R. Barnicote MSc – though if he'd known they were going to elect The Feelie he might have thought twice about democracy. He's not really a Fascist, old Bandicoot, just authoritarian. Same thing, really. God knows why anyone wanted to put up a statue in the quad, anyway; perhaps they hoped to encourage Art Appreciation from an early age – in which case they succeeded – but Gerry has always been very proprietorial about it (I'm beginning to use words I didn't know I knew. Great brain exercise, this diary kick), being indignant when he heard any of us being rude about it. It's very difficult *not* to be rude about it, it's so . . . rude.

I've been thinking about that sperm again – the one that made it to the top, as it were. Is it still *there*? Here, I mean, in me. Or has it all been regenerated? I seem to remember from biology lessons that we replace all our cells every seven years. In which case I must be like George Washington's axe, the one in the museum: new haft, new blade, but otherwise the original, genuine axe. Or Old Number One.

If I'd started this diary sooner we'd have had the saga of Old Number One, the great Speed Six racing Bentley that crashed at Brooklands in 1932. The case went to the High Court – was it the real Old Number One or had it been so rebuilt that there was only a couple of the original screws and a floorboard left? The whole thing was down to money, of course. Was it worth a fortune – or only a small fortune? The judge said that it didn't matter if it had been rebuilt, it was still Old Number One, so I reckon I can asume that *my* Old Number One is still in there somewhere.

Or is this sexist? Isn't the egg as much entitled to call itself Old Number One? Are sperm male anyway? I'll have to think about this.

Meanwhile, everything goes on as normal. It's eerie in a way. Things shouldn't be going on as normal. Yesterday it was brink-talk, today (and I was right, it isn't funny) the Iraqis are putting foreign civilians near military installations. *Why* hasn't Parliament been recalled? I can't remember when the Prime Minister was so quiet. Haven't seen her for *days*. (I'm not complaining.)

Been thinking a lot about wars and history – which is mainly wars. All my life I've thought of this century as one war after another, Second Boer War, World War One, Spanish Civil, World War Two, Korea, Cold War, Vietnam, Falklands, but I bet in a century or so the history books will just refer to The World War 1914-1989, or maybe, Sporadic Hostilities. And now this. But if you didn't watch the News you wouldn't know anything was happening, it's business as usual – sitcoms, game shows, old movies, summer repeats and soaps.

Geoff and I and Dan Campion are going to watch *The Phantom of the Opera* on Sunday, not the musical, a new version for the telly – see, even *I* can't keep my mind on the bloody Gulf, and I'm *trying*. I keep thinking about the Guildford Four and the Birmingham Six and the Maguires, and what's for dinner. I bet the Irish have got more to worry about than Iraq.

APRIL 4TH 1982 SUNDAY

The Defence Secretary, John Nott, says we are preparing for war with Argentina, but what exactly, I wonder, does 'preparing for war' mean? In ports, garrison towns and air bases I imagine that whole populations feel involved, especially where relatives of military personnel are concerned, but the rest of us have to go on exactly as usual. Once upon a time I suppose we would all have turned out to line the streets and wave flags as the troops marched by. I would hesitate to describe the national mood as apathetic and grass roots feeling must be that brutal aggression cannot be disregarded. Perhaps all this will revive the sense of what it means to be British, slow to anger but terrible when roused! Time will tell.

The United States is prepared to support us 'in the last military resort'. 'Always the last to join in,' my father said, 'and then they walk off claiming they've won.' 'I don't see the world queuing up to join this party,' said my mother.

Here in Calderley the news, which has even merited attention on local television, is a murder. As is well known, in the majority of such crimes the assailant is closely connected to the victim, often a member of the family. There have been relatively few murders in our immediate vicinity but such as there are have proved to be of this routine nature, taking place either before witnesses or in such circumstances that the police are in no doubt as to the identity of the killer. Our murder, however, appears to be a genuine 'whodunnit' as the man's identity is unknown. Unfortunately I was in the kitchen at the time (of the bulletin, not the murder!) so missed the details. I had just returned from a meeting of our Capsule Committee. Jo-Ann Rugg and Mark Lovell failed to attend but the others remain committed – no pun intended! Jon Lo suggested that we all write 'letters to the future' and the motion was carried. Lucy Ashton confided to me as we cycled home that she had been inclined to abstain as she was not at all sure it was a good idea.

'Are we going to vet the letters?' she said. 'Otherwise people might put in all sorts of things about each other and give the wrong impression.'

'It will all be the same in a hundred years,' I said. I did sympathize, however, as the letters will not be confined to the committee but may come from anyone in the Upper Sixth, as will other contributions. Given that the sixth form involves 63 people of widely differing attitudes (of whom 35 are Upper Sixth) there is no certainty that they will all treat the project with equal seriousness.

Personally I would imagine that you, our readers, will be able to draw your own conclusions about the writers of those letters. If they exist you may have read them already!

Sunday 19.8.90

I've left Geoff and friends in front of the telly watching a war film, the Sunday afternoon explosion slot. Last week it was Krakatoa, today it's 1940-something, the war in the Pacific, blasting the Japanese out of the air or out of the water and off the beach.

Don't get me wrong, I *love* explosions. When I was a kid my ambition was to be the person who detonates the dynamite to blow up old cooling towers and new blocks of flats. But right now I don't see how anyone can think of war as entertainment, especially war at sea. In the Gulf, the Americans have been firing shots across bows. Iraq calls it piracy – well, it would, wouldn't it?

I've just looked at what I've written, 'Well, it would, wouldn't it?' Who am I asking? No, mustn't start doing that, I'll get self-conscious again. When I started this diary I wrote down the first things that came into my head, just to get going, but it seems to be the only way to *keep* going. Every time I come up here and open this book I have in mind a whole lot of things I want to write about the international situation, but it always gets swamped by all this *trivia*.

For instance

I mean, what I wanted to write about was the United Nations, which is actually united for the first time I can remember. Fifteen votes, no dissent, no abstentions, condemning Iraq's threats to harm foreigners who have all been assembled at three hotels and are being moved to military installations. If that isn't using them as hostages, what is? But here I am, eight lines from the bottom of the page and I still haven't written anything worth saying. Perhaps I just have a hopelessly trivial mind.

There's so much I could write if my thoughts didn't keep getting in the way. I *know* what I'm thinking – why do I have this urge to see it on paper?

There has been another IRA bomb in Northern Ireland, in Soweto there is murderous fighting between ANC supporters and the Zulu Inkatha supporters, with Terreblanche and his neo-Nazis stirring up the whites on the sidelines. These things would have been headlines a month ago and now they're crowded out into second or third place. And still the cricket goes on, and the athletics meetings – and the football. Football *again*. Already.

Why aren't we more afraid?

Surely we didn't poodle on as usual when the last war (WWII) broke out? Ah! Now we're on to something, I've read about this. When WWII began everyone was sure that Germany would immediately bomb London. And it could have – Germany is so close. But the Gulf is a long way away. Iraq has no nuclear warheads, it can't reach us. I wonder if that is why everyone is piling into Saddam Hussein now, before he does go nuclear. It was the same with the Falklands, I suppose. Too far away to threaten us personally. I was only nine at the time but I can still remember, I never felt afraid. It was all so far away. I was much more afraid of the Russians.

The Middle East isn't so very far away and there's more at stake this time than a couple of islands and an old whaling station. All right, I know the Falklanders don't see it that way, but it was a lot more straightforward. The Falklands didn't have any oil, for a start.

According to today's paper, war looks inevitable.

If anyone ever sees this

It's odd, I can't get rid of the feeling that somebody *might* see it one day, and say, who did he think he was, this Hugh Marshall, writing down his fatuous opinions? Well, whoever you are, I don't think I'm anybody in particular but most of my friends are on holiday and I don't have anyone to talk to. It's like comforting to know that I can write everything down; I almost look forward to coming up here and sitting alone for a bit, and *thinking* and writing.

I've just looked back at page 1 where I was wittering on about Mass Observation and keeping a record of day-to-day events. A fat lot of good this would be to Mass Observation. All I've set down of day-to-day interest is my name, my brothers' names and their A-level results. Oh yes, and you know my age (I was born at 10 am.). Apart from that I might be living on another planet like that Cabinet Minister I was sneering at. Well, if not on a different planet, in Limbo.

I mean, can you guess where I live, what my parents are like? Who the neighbours are, or my friends? Absolute egotism – this time I *mean* egotism. I. I. I. No one exists in this diary unless *I* allow them to.

I'm not really like this.

APRIL 5TH 1982 MONDAY

The Task Force sails today from Plymouth – what echoes of ancient warfare that stirs. Drake and the Armada. This too is an Armada; forty vessels comprising nuclear submarines, destroyers and frigates etc., two aircraft carriers, one assault ship and one thousand marines. The Foreign Secretary and the Defence Secretary have faced violent criticism for not foreseeing the invasion and preventing it – such as acting when South Georgia was invaded two weeks ago. The obvious riposte is that if we were so unprepared, how can we muster and dispatch the Task Force so rapidly?

Strict regulations have been imposed upon the Falkland Islanders by the army of occupation. They must stay indoors on pain of fifteen days' imprisonment. Thirty days for making rude gestures and sixty days for showing disrespect for the Argentinian flag. British currency is no longer valid.

In spite of all this 'our' murder displaces all international news on the front page of the local paper. The victim is a middle-aged man who was found battered to death in the car park of the Duke of York. The car park was empty, the victim had no identification on him and no one had reported him missing. Since this could happen to anyone – not the murder but being temporarily alone in a strange town with no identification, myself included, none of this strikes me as particularly mysterious, but the *Calderley Chronicle* behaves as though it were the crime of the century! It occupied the entire front page excluding advertisements, and half of page two. The Falklands were pushed to the centre pages.

I shall, of course, record any progress made in the police investigation, as it may afford you some amusement when you contemplate our antiquated forensic procedures!

At home this evening I discussed the Time Capsule with my parents. My father, Anthony Ansell Marshall is, at the time of writing, manager of a local electronic installation company; my mother, Elizabeth Rosemary Marshall, née Seward, is a housewife. I understand from 'feminist' friends that this is considered a term of abuse these days, but with three children, two of them still at primary school, it seems eminently sensible to remain at home. She can no doubt resume working as an infant school teacher when Geoffrey and Hugh are older. It is not as though she will have lost touch in the interim. Infants are infants.

I mention my parents because both Marshall and Seward are old Calderley families. This implies that they are landed gentry which, of course, is not the case! Rather it suggests historical inertia. It would be interesting to know, as you know, if there are still Marshalls and Sewards in Calderley in 2082.

Geoffrey, the elder of my two brothers, is extremely fit and active. Hugh however is severely asthmatic and was often gravely ill in his early childhood. Now he is responding to treatment but we have been warned that the illness may return in his late teens. Does it sound very callous if I wonder whether he will live and marry and father children of his own?

I do hope that our great-grandchildren are among those who are reading this.

Monday 20.8.90

OK, come clean. It's Evelyn I'm missing.

I've been looking at that for *half an hour*, wondering whether to go on, genuinely come clean and write down what I'm really thinking and feeling. Well, I'm not going to write down what I'm *feeling*, I mean, there are limits, this is a family newspaper etc. etc. I can't speak to her again till Thursday, in fact, when I began this diary last week I'd just rung her up, but we're rationed. One week she rings me, one week I ring her. Her turn this week. Rationing! Ah, cruel fate.

It's not fate, it's the cost of a phone call to Boston Mass. Mum doesn't listen at the door but I know she watches the clock – I have to time the calls. So does Eve. (I wonder why I didn't mention her last Thursday. Was I really hoping to keep her out of it?) I said I'd pay for the calls but Mum said don't be daft you'd be bankrupt in a week. Bank-rupt. Bank rupture. Bank broken. Break the bank. How odd. I never thought of that before.

She's right. What they pay me for mornings at the garden centre wouldn't cover the cost of many transatlantic phone calls. Geoff put on a Monty Python Yorkshire accent and said, 'Eh, lad, that's what comes of moving out of thy class. If tha must muck around wi' brass . . .' How was I to know her old man was a property developer? Everyone looks the same round the back of the Corn Exchange at midnight. Her stepmother, who is really nice, said why didn't I fly out to join them for a couple of weeks? Ho ho. I said I had too much work to do, which was the honest truth. Marty (step-ma) believed me. I really don't think the *cost* had occurred to her. I don't know why they make Eve ration her calls. Perhaps they think it's good for her soul to learn how the other half lives.

The other 99.5%, I should have said.

Of course, I could be writing to Eve instead of scribbling this rubbish – no I couldn't, I'd be tongue-tied. Pen-tied. I can't even write much here.

Oh, I could.

I can't.

Another half hour. Suddenly remembered my last diary. I know I kicked off this one by saying I'd never kept a diary before, which is true, but I did possess one once. Gerald gave it to me for Christmas 1987. Just the sort of prat present he *would* give me, too.

It had one entry: January The First 1988. MUST LOSE MY VIRGINITY. I was fourteen.

I can't remember if it was an outburst of frustrated lust or a New Year's resolution, but whichever it was, I had to wait another two years.

Two and a half, nearly.

10.5.90. It wasn't Evelyn. Don't tell her. I wish it had been.

I wasn't her first, either.

I don't screw around.

I don't have to tell *you* that.

I sent her a card on Saturday which I got at the same time that I bought Gerry's. Evelyn's was a print of Picasso's 'Woman in a Chemise' because it reminds me of her – not the face. Although it is a *face*, not like some of his later ones with both eyes on the same side like a turbot.

Gerry's card was the rudest I could find. 'What's the

score?' it said on the outside, and inside, this photograph of a big hairy rugger bugger with a pop-up
jockstrap. He hates that kind of thing. I wouldn't
actually want to receive it, either. But the last time he
was home he was so snotty about one of my friends –
Tassy, and she *is* just a friend – that if I was going to
annoy him I might as well do it properly, though just
telling him about The Feelie will probably do the job
. . . The thought of them moving his precious lump of
rock.

Well, he ought to have remembered my birthday. I
always remember his. He'd probably have given me an
address book. I mean, fancy giving a fourteen-year-old
a *desk* diary.

I've been so fed up today I haven't seen or heard the
News or even looked at the paper. Will nip down and
look at BBC News at 9 o'clock though we usually
watch ITN. Must keep you up to date.

Keep *who* up to date?

So:

President Bush has just used the word 'hostages' for
the first time.

Foreign nationals from countries like Sweden and
Switzerland which haven't joined the arms build-up in
Saudi and the Gulf are being allowed to leave Iraq and
Kuwait, but 123 Britons in Kuwait have been rounded
up and moved to military installations as human
shields.

Jordan is being swamped with refugees. I've always
known vaguely where all these countries are but when
I looked at the map and saw exactly where Jordan is –
and how small it is – I could see what they meant by
swamped.

The Foreign Secretary called the internment of

'hostages' repulsive and illegal. *Illegal?* War's legal, I suppose. It suddenly struck me; war *is* legal. It has rules. It even has a name. W A R. That's obscene.

The Russians have said that Iraq should let all foreign nationals leave. They are calling for a negotiated settlement. They say they are ready to be mediators. This would have been totally incredible a couple of years ago – last year, even.

I noted all this down on the edge of the *Guardian*.

Right at the bottom of the front page, in the left-hand corner under News in Brief, there was a little bit about Arthur Scargill. 6 lines. More on page 20. Page 20 – *Arthur Scargill!* That says it all.

After the News there was a play, then *Come Dancing*. And here I am sending silly cards to people and counting the hours till Thursday. A lot of people don't even have hours to count, probably.

APRIL 6TH 1982 TUESDAY

First of all, our murder. The dead man's vehicle has been located in the car park of another pub, the Lamb and Flag, about a mile away at the other end of town. An unnamed witness saw him leaving it there on Saturday afternoon. The victim has not been named either and it seems that the car had been stolen. Perhaps this will turn out to be what we call a 'gangland killing' though Calderley can scarcely be described as 'gangland'! This morning I met Jo-Ann outside the public library (one would hardly expect to meet Jo-Ann *in* the library!) and reminded her that she had missed the committee meeting on Saturday evening. She said she was very sorry but that she'd had to meet a friend. Jo-Ann's social life has always taken precedence over her commitments (another pun. Tut!). I was rather surprised when she was voted on to the committee but she is a very popular girl for all the usual reasons. She said she thought Mark Lovell had a virus infection, which accounts for *his* absence.

Lord Carrington, the Foreign Secretary, resigned last night. On television Mrs Thatcher refuses to say whether or not we are at war, all that matters is that we recover those islands! An ITN survey says 70% of Britons favour the sinking of Argentine ships, 41% favour the use of military force, 69% favour putting at risk the lives of British Armed Forces to regain control. I would have thought that having your life put at risk was all part of being in the Armed Forces, after all, one is armed! Britain wants EEC partners to join in putting diplomatic and economic pressure on Argentina. I think personally that Armed Might is the only pressure that Galtieri will understand.

In the Gulf War Saudi Arabia and Kuwait have called for aid to Iraq in defeating Iran.

Ian Paisley, the Ulster Unionist, has attacked James Prior's initiative for power-sharing in Northern Ireland and in Poland the martial law authorities have blamed the country's slump on Solidarity.

Our new Foreign Secretary is Francis Pym.

Tuesday 21.8.90

The garden centre was busy this morning. It must be the weather. Since the drought broke people are starting to think about their gardens again. Dad was out dead-heading roses when I left for work.

Sometimes I think I'd happily chuck university and A-levels and work there full-time, or go in for horticulture, or just get a job with the council. I used to wish I was one of those blokes who look after the plants on roundabouts. When I was little I used to think that must be a lovely job, rather like living on a desert island, all the traffic roaring round and hooting, and me marooned in the middle with the flowers. I still do think it, sometimes.

Some of the blokes are girls these days. I noticed one on the roundabout on the ring road this morning as I was cycling to work. She was with Jason Ames who is an old mate of Gerry's from school. Well, a contemporary – I don't think that Gerry would use the word mate and has probably forgotten that he used to knock around with Jason. I didn't know Jason worked for the council – he was with a breakdown recovery outfit last time I saw him and before that he was a security guard in the Chiltern Centre. Poacher turned gamekeeper, Mum said when she saw him.

No way would I want to be marooned on a desert island with Jason Ames, even if it was only a council roundabout.

Because we were so busy I spent most of the morning in the coffee shop which has more to do with hamburgers and microwaves than coffee. When I started working there they didn't have the microwave, but now it's pinging away all the time at regular intervals like Chinese water torture. I wasn't sorry when it was time to swap with Steve and go out to hose down the roses. We were lucky with the drought. The hosepipe ban had only been in force for a few days when the rains came – sounds sort of tropical, doesn't it? The Calderley Monsoon Season. For all I know there's still a hosepipe ban. Perhaps the garden centre has a special dispensation. The council seems to, or else it just doesn't care. Jason had a hose.

Someone left a copy of the *Mirror* in the shop so I took it to read during my coffee break. I couldn't believe the headline: WE'LL EAT YOUR PILOTS. I thought it was a joke like the famous one in the *Sun* a few years back: FREDDIE STARR ATE MY HAMSTER. In our paper it was more like, 'If any of your pilots are shot down they will be instantly devoured'. I didn't take it literally. Did the Iraqis *mean* it literally?

There was more about the Middle East inside, daring escapes and so on, but otherwise it was the usual stuff:

FROM HOLLYWOOD HELL TO HAPPINESS

GUNMAN KIDNAPS GRAN, 62

RAT OF THE ROVERS IS BACK
(Coronation Street)

FLIPPING HELL (dolphins)

REFORM SCHOOL TOTS BORN
TO BE CROOKS!

Politicians aren't the only ones on a different planet.

When I went back indoors there was this little old lady sitting with her coffee, reading the *Daily Star*. I leaned on the counter and read the front page while she was stuck into the middle. The type was so huge I could see it from the other end of the shop.

ROUND 'EM ALL UP.

'EM was the Iraqis, all the Iraqis in Britain. The *Star* wants them interned, I suppose, in case they start a terrorist movement here – which they may do, for all I know. Can't expect the average Iraqi-in-the-street to see the Gulf in the same way as the average Brit-in-the-street. But you can imagine what might happen. It seems to me that Iraqis look exactly the same as everyone else from the Middle East. Being Arab-looking at the moment must be like having an Irish accent after the IRA have bombed a barracks. They must feel so threatened, Irish people in England, whether or not they have Republican Sympathies. What *are* Republican Sympathies anyway? I think I have Republican Sympathies myself, but that doesn't mean I support terrorism. I just don't think we should be in Ireland. I don't think we should *ever* have been in Ireland, though it's no good bitching about something that started six hundred years ago.

Why can't we all just stay at home? *Why* are we involved in the Middle East anyway?

Oil.

Who was the lunatic who invented the internal combustion engine?

Today is the fiftieth anniversary of the death of Leon Trotsky. Just thought you'd like to know.

APRIL 7TH 1982 WEDNESDAY

I spent most of today revising. This will be my – and most of my friends' – schedule for the holiday although it lasts only two weeks. However we shall, I hope, all devote some thought to the Time Capsule. Will Thomson has suggested that a video tape should be made of a typical day at school. I do not know if any of us will be able to do this but perhaps one of the Lower Sixth, unhampered by the threat of exams, will be able to make the recording with the assistance of Mr Morris, the teacher in charge of resources.

I wonder what kind of educational system you will be enjoying in 2082? I am sure it will be far superior to ours and with a far greater bias towards science and technology. Also, I trust, the liberal egalitarianism that has for decades undermined our schools will have been long laid to rest. Earlier I referred to this establishment as a 'comprehensive school'. I realize now that this may require elucidation. The comprehensive element is that it comprises the two kinds of school that it was intended to replace: 'grammar' for the most able students and 'secondary' for the less academically gifted.

It seems to me that this system has not succeeded in its aims. Ours was originally a grammar school and Mercery Lane, nearby, was a secondary modern. Now both are comprehensive schools. There are many students in this school who would have been far happier, I think, at a school such as Mercery Lane once was, where they were not daily in the company of the academically ambitious. Several disruptive elements have had to be removed from the school in the past year.

After reading this you are probably eager to move on to global matters, but I did promise you a commentary on local concerns and I think we must qualify as a local concern! And, on a global scale, nothing much is going on at the moment. The Fleet is still on its way to the Falklands, but there is little information available about what will happen when it gets there, in an estimated two weeks. The Argentinians predict that the Task Force will arrive on April 20th, but they claim that 'Las Malvinas', as they call the Falklands, are impregnable. By the time the Fleet arrives they will have increased their troop numbers from 5,000 to 7,000 or possibly, ultimately to 20,000.

The United States and other countries have offered to mediate, but Mrs Thatcher insists, rightly, that General Galtieri must withdraw his forces before any talks commence. The Soviet Union of course blames *us* for the invasion, but this is just the reaction one would expect!

In the House of Commons Labour, exploiting the situation with a cynicism verging on treachery, has called for the Prime Minister's resignation over the Government's 'mishandling' of the crisis.

The Americans have ruled out a freeze on nuclear stockpiling. It is hard to see how they could do otherwise in the current international climate!

Wednesday 22.8.90

Another birthday; the Fax Bureau this time, two years old and going strong. There's a party there this evening. I said I'd look in, and I did. One look was enough, but I stayed half an hour, to please Mum. She and Dad were there, of course, and Barbara who runs the bureau with Mum, and Barbara's new old man and a lot of friends of all of them. Geoff fixed up sound equipment so they could dance. Imagine – dancing in a Fax Bureau. They couldn't close it, naturally. It's usually open till 11.30 so Mum and Barbara are taking it in turns to watch the front office, for customers. They have a lot of regulars – all the small local businesses that haven't gone bust yet. Pauline who works there is looking after the machine. I don't know what happens if they all get pissed – some very strange messages will be going out. That is, the messages will be OK but they may turn up in some very odd places.

I don't know why I said 'of course' Dad was there. He usually steers clear of the bureau and never shows the slightest interest in it when Mum wants to talk. I think it's Barbara who gets up his nose, to tell the truth, and her husband's a pig.

I left when Geoff started dancing with Pauline. Geoff dancing looks like Bill Wyman playing bass. He stands there completely motionless and completely expressionless; just hangs onto the lady and lets her hop about.

And also: 'This day was our good King Richard piteously slain and murdered; to the great heaviness of this city', as they said in York in 1485. Richard

Plantagenet, Richard III, the last English king of England, died at the Battle of Bosworth 505 years ago today. Someone puts a notice in the *In Memoriam* every year on his behalf, as if he'd died quite recently. I like that.

It's no good wondering what would have happened if he'd won at Bosworth. There'd have been no Tudors, for a start, no Henry VIII, Anne Boleyn would have died in bed and we'd all be Catholics.

Still, if he had won, Shakespeare wouldn't have written *Richard III*, the first creature feature; well, actually, he'd have written it, but it would have been all about what a great bloke Good King Dick was.

Excuse me. The phone . . .

Ah – my hand was shaking when I wrote that, look how the writing wobbles. I thought for a moment – well, until I got down to the phone – that Evelyn might be ringing a day early, but I didn't say 'Hello sexy' when I picked up the receiver which was just as well, because it was Gerry.

I couldn't believe it. He *never* rings. I expect he calls Mum and Dad *occasionally* but he doesn't live here any more so I suppose he forgets us for months at a time. This isn't his *home* now, so I don't imagine he misses it, or us. Anyway, it was *me* he was ringing.

'Ha!' I said. 'Guilty conscience, Bro?'

'No. Why?' He sounded really taken aback.

Me: My birthday, you cad.

G: Oh, God, sorry about that. (Not only had he forgotten about it, he'd forgotten he'd forgotten about it.)

Me (*Very fraternal*): What are you ringing for, then?

G (*Sort of mumbling*): It's about thrust.

Me: You what?

G: Thrust 15 . . . in your letter. The sculpture.
Jeez! The Feelie.

Me: Thrust 15? Is that what it's called? Why 15?

G: I think it was one of a series. Look, has it been moved yet?

Me: I don't know. It was still there at the end of term. (I'm sure of that because I'd thought of something new and inventive to do with the traffic cone.)

G: Well, can you check? I mean, they haven't started digging yet, have they?

Me: I don't know. I don't spend all my spare time hanging around the place (like he used to, for instance). Look, they aren't going to break it up.

G: What?

Me: The Feelie.

G: The *what*?

Me: Thrust 15. It's just going to be shifted across to the rose bed in front of the main door.

And Gerry said, 'Bugger the sculpture – *have they started digging?*'

I said, 'I don't know, I told you. I saw a JCB going up Foundry Hill at the weekend.'

He sounded as if he were imploding. 'Can you go and find out?'

I said not bloody likely, it was half past nine and pitch dark.

'Well, go in the morning, will you?' he said. 'Go and look. It's important.'

'Ask nicely,' I said.

He yelled, 'For Christ's sake, just do it!' so I promised I would. I'll make a detour on the way to work.

Very weird. I've never known him lose his rag before in his life. A cool dude, our Gerald.

No, a cold fish, that's more like it.

Just went down to look at the 10 o'clock News.
Doesn't seem to have changed much since teatime.
Bush has called up his reserves (army). British nationals
are being rounded up at gun-point in Kuwait. There
was a lot about relatives waiting for news.

I can't begin to imagine what it's like for them,
waiting, not knowing what's happening. And I've
tried imagining what it must be like out there, trapped,
frightened, with the threat of shooting and chemical
warfare.

I can't imagine it.

Meanwhile, back at the ranch, the Fax Bureau is
celebrating its second birthday and everybody's
getting drunk. Gerald's only worried about whether
someone's going to move his scabby sculpture – we
were talking for nearly five minutes and he never
mentioned the Gulf once. Still, the Swiss aren't really
involved. Perhaps it doesn't make headlines over there.

Gerry said once that everybody in Switzerland has a
nuclear fall-out shelter.

Big deal.

They keep interviewing the Iraqi ambassador in
London, asking him about the British who are being
held prisoner. Whatever is said to him, he just answers,
'They are not prisoners, they are our guests.'

You can see that the words mean nothing and he
knows they mean nothing. He doesn't even look at the
camera.

APRIL 8TH 1982 THURSDAY

We are enduring, or enjoying, an hiatus until the Task Force arrives in the South Atlantic, when it will establish a blockade around the Falkland Islands to prevent the army of occupation importing supplies from the mainland of Argentina. The Government has announced that it has authorized the Navy to sink Argentinian warships and 'naval auxiliaries' inside a 200 mile radius around the Falklands, starting at 4 am. on Easter Monday – in four days' time. Meanwhile France and West Germany have joined in an arms embargo to Argentina and the US Secretary of State (their foreign minister, as it were) Alexander Haig is flying in to Downing Street this morning for talks, before going on to Buenos Aires.

One hundred thousand Britons in Argentina have urged a peaceful settlement but here at home a new political force has emerged, The British National Party, calling for the mass hanging of the 'traitors' responsible for the crisis. I suppose they mean MPs. I don't think I should go as far as that, but I would have thought that after what happened with Hitler, appeasement should be far from our minds! I mentioned this at dinner. My mother said, 'You think Haig's going to come back from Buenos Aires waving a bit of paper and offering peace in our time?' I replied that the British in Argentina *would* want a peaceful solution, wouldn't they, out of self-interest if nothing else.

'Nobody's going to blow your head off, though, are they?' my mother said.

The *Calderley Chronicle* has, of course, managed to

find a local angle on the crisis: AGONY OF
FALKLANDS MUM. For a day or two there has been
no mention of our murder. The victim remains
unidentified. Even though the car was stolen he was
not, presumably, an habitual thief or the police would
have had a record of his fingerprints.

As I said earlier, your forensic methods will be far in
advance of ours and it is quite possible that finger-
printing will be a thing of the past when you read this!

The committee met again this evening. All were
present except Mark Lovell who is still unwell. We
discussed the various successes we had met with in
canvassing for contributions for the Time Capsule and
unanimously regretted that we had not thought of it
sooner, before the end of term, when we could have
called the whole year together for a meeting.

Suggestions so far are:

Letters to the Future.

Some seeds – to see if you can germinate them.

A poster depicting 'Adam and the Ants'.

A video tape of some kind.

An audio tape of some kind.

A collection of ephemera (bus and train tickets,
airline tickets, savings coupons, theatre programmes,
book reviews).

An autograph of Peter Shilton the celebrated
goalkeeper.

A school report (Lucy Ashton and William Sargent
have offered theirs as extreme examples of the genre).

The Top Twenty. (You may find this totally
mystifying when you read it. The Top Twenty is a list
of the best-selling popular songs of the week. I should
have mentioned above that 'Adam and the Ants' are a
'pop group', that is, a band of musicians, sometimes

genuinely talented, who perform and often write the popular tunes of the Top Twenty.

An LP. (This is a long-playing gramophone record, an artefact which you may no longer have the equipment to play although a museum might be able to help!)

Timothy Finch offered what he described as a 'treasured' Rolling Stones album, but this was vetoed on the grounds that the Rolling Stones are already history and did not accurately reflect today's interests.

Robert Whiting suggested that we should ask you if flares have come back into fashion. If they have not you may like to know that these were a particularly repulsive form of trousers prevalent in the 1970s.

Naseem Amin says that the poster of 'Adam and the Ants' might give people the wrong idea of what we look like in 1982. If we include it, rest assured that Adam and the Ants were not typical, particularly the one with the stripes on his face.

Jo-Ann apologized for missing the last meeting and said that if her parents asked any of us where she had been that evening not to reveal that she had not been with us. It will probably seem strange to you that a young woman of eighteen should have to account for her whereabouts to her parents. It seems strange to us. I suspect that those of you reading this will have had the vote from the age of fourteen!

Thursday 23.8.90

Lunchtime. Just home from Chandler's. Forgot to look in at school on the way this morning, so I went back that way.

Signs of activity. The JCB has been at work but only between the science wing and the gate. There are lots of orange tapes on stakes round the quadrangle and a couple of Portakabins have arrived. The quad looks like Stonehenge, with great stacks of bricks and Thermolite blocks. The Feelie is still there. While I was looking at it the Head came out of the front door with a load of box files. He looked surprised to see me. I was quite surprised to see him. He was wearing a track suit. Usually he goes round in a tweed three-piece that looks as if it was hewn out of millstone grit.

But *I* was formal. 'Sir,' I said, 'do you know what's going to happen to Thrust 15?'

'*What?*' he said.

I pointed. I hadn't the nerve to say it again.

'That?' he said. 'Thrust 15? Is that what you call it?'

'No,' I said, and I saw that he was grinning, so I told him. 'We call it The Feelie.'

'We call it the Hand of Ken,' he said, 'in honour of a former Education Secretary. In winter the sun sets behind it and casts a threatening shadow over the staff room,' which surprised me a bit, coming from him, I mean.

'Are they going to move it?' I know they are, but I didn't want to give too much away.

'Perhaps they'll break it up for hard core,' he said, rather wistfully. 'No, the contractors are bringing a crane to shift it next week. Why, do you want it? Take it, do.'

'My brother was asking about it,' I said. 'Not Geoff, Gerald. He was before your time. I think he had something to do with it.'

'I can't imagine what,' said Bandicoot, and gave it a nasty look. 'Why's it there, anyway?'

'I'll ask him,' I said. I'd have thought he'd know, but I suppose he's got better things to do than make inquiries about works of art, even if they are stuck outside his office. No one seems to know anything about The Quatermass Experiment either, which is a large greenish painting in the entrance hall.

'Oh, well, see you in September,' he said. 'I'm off to the sillies tomorrow.'

After he'd gone I realized he meant the Scilly Isles. I thought he'd come off his trolley, for a moment.

Geoff was bumming around the garden when I got in, going through the motions of weeding the onion bed and smoking something very fragrant in a *pipe*. I think he's getting in training for Durham, University of. Mum tried to persuade him to take a year off and see life after A-levels but he wouldn't. Gerry was going to Israel, I think, but he never did. No one in their right mind would go to Israel now, not to see life. Rather the reverse.

I asked Geoff if he'd seen the News and he said yes, but nothing had happened except that the American reserves were being called up, which I knew, and all the British in Kuwait had been accounted for. I said, 'Aren't you worried?'

'Oh, stuff it,' he said. 'I grew up having nightmares about the Bomb. As soon as that's over with we get all this. I dunno . . .'

7 pm. I used to have nightmares about the Bomb, right from when I was tiny. One of them was so vivid I still remember it. I was in the back garden, only like things are in dreams, it was about a mile long and just grass, with a hedge at the end, a horrible ratty scraggy hedge of thorn bushes. No houses around, like there really are, in fact I don't think even our house was there. I was on my own, near the hedge, and it was getting dark. Then suddenly these missiles flew over. They were only a few metres above my head and absolutely silent. That's what I remember most. I *felt* them go over, very slowly, but I didn't hear anything. There were three of them. Then there was a sort of rush and they got faster and disappeared over the hedge. I knew they had landed and suddenly I wasn't on my own any more. There were several people, grown-ups, standing about, and we all went round the hedge to have a look.

On the other side was what looked like a big compost heap, smoking a bit (I realized afterwards that I was remembering a pile of manure I'd seen steaming when we were on holiday in Norfolk) and I was just feeling relieved that there hadn't been an explosion when somebody said, 'You don't feel the effects for years,' and immediately it *was* years later, and I was somewhere indoors, standing by a table. There was an arm on the table – well, just a bone really, with fingers, and I knew that it was *my* arm. That was when I woke up.

Don't worry. I'm not going to start writing my dreams down. I never seem to remember them, anyway, these days.

I only wrote that because I'm killing time waiting for Evelyn to ring. It's about 2 o'clock in Boston. I don't know if she has to wait for the cheap rate like I do. Perhaps they don't have one over there.

Come on, Eve!

Aha!

It was Gerry. He was *extremely* anxious. I told him that The Feelie is due to be moved next week. 'When?' he says. 'Well, it won't be Monday,' I said. 'That's the Bank Holiday.'

There was a long pause. 'You still there, Bro?' I said. I could hear him breathing. At last he said, 'Look, I'm going to take you into my confidence.'

'Gee, thanks,' I said. 'Is there room?'

'Look!' (Why do people say 'look' on the phone?) 'I don't suppose you remember this but when the sculpture was installed in '82, a group of us buried a Time Capsule under it.'

'That'll be interesting,' I said politely. I wouldn't have thought that Gerry would ever get involved in anything interesting. Gerald 'Interesting' Marshall. 'Do you want me to ask them to keep it for you?'

'Who?'

'The contractors, when they dig it up.'

There was another bout of heavy breathing, and then he said, 'No, I want *you* to dig it up.'

'Look,' I said (you can't help it, actually), 'I told you, there's a JCB. You don't need puny Hugh.'

Oh, but he does need puny Hugh. Apparently the capsule is one of those boxes that films are sent out in, and although they are very strong they aren't built to withstand a JCB crashing through the roof.

'How far down is it?' I said, and he said that the concrete slab that The Feelie stands on is 30 cm thick, much of it in the ground, and the capsule is (he thinks!)

90 cm below that. Or maybe a hundred.

'For God's sake,' I said, 'anyone would think you were burying a corpse. Why didn't you just shove it under the slab?'

'Look,' he said, 'we didn't think Thrust 15 would be moved, but, you know, concrete can split. We didn't want anyone finding it by accident. That capsule was meant to be buried for a hundred years.'

APRIL 9TH 1982 GOOD FRIDAY

In the Falklands conflict the United States has proposed a multi-national peace-keeping force, which sounds very fine, but since the peace has already been breached I cannot, myself, see what purpose it would serve. The Common Market, in typical fashion, is holding back over implementing trade sanctions. Are they our allies or not? The Soviet Union has called the Task Force a threat to world peace, which is only to be expected. World peace has already been threatened, and not by the United Kingdom!

The Israeli ceasefire across the Lebanese border has also been threatened. Suddenly the Middle East seems very unimportant. It goes without saying that we shall drive the Argentinians out of the Falklands, but it is hard to imagine what will happen in the Gulf. And will the Palestinian Question have been solved by 2082?

I feel as if I have received a visit from a revenant! On a previous page I referred to persons who had been excluded from school for various reasons. One of these people was a boy of my own age called Jason Ames, who was actually expelled on suspicion of drug-taking, although he already had a history of petty crime, mainly involving vehicles, particularly batteries.

This morning Jason appeared at the house as I was leaving and asked to have a word with me. As I was on my way to the office to deliver my father's briefcase that he had left at home (he often works on holidays and in the evenings) I suggested he came with me. We both had bicycles. We exchanged pleasantries as we

rode and had covered about half the distance before he
explained what he wanted. He had, he said, heard
about the Time Capsule from Jo-Ann Rugg. Could
anyone join, he said.

I pointed out that it was not really a matter of
joining.

'It's not just a school thing, then,' he said.

I pointed out that in a sense it *was* a school thing
because the sculpture had been given to the school and
all those concerned with the Time Capsule were in the
Upper Sixth.

'Well, I'd have been in the Upper Sixth if I'd stayed,'
he said.

I forebore to remind him why he had not stayed. I
asked why he wanted to be involved.

'Old times' sake,' he said. 'I'd like to make a gesture
to the future too.'

I asked him what he had in mind.

'I could dig the hole for a start,' he said. 'I'm grave-
digging for the council right now, aren't I? I'm *used* to
digging holes. And maybe I could write something for
you about grave-digging – you know, late twentieth-
century burial customs.'

It's easy to forget, seeing Jason, that he is as
intelligent as the rest of us. I thanked him for his offer,
particularly with regard to the hole.

'It'll be a pleasure,' he said. 'How deep do you want
it? When would you like me to start? Tonight?'

I explained that the statue is not due to be erected
until May 5th, so this would be a little premature. I also
told him about my diary of local and world events. 'It
will be a record of an entire month,' I said. 'I don't
intend to abandon it after eight days,' and I pointed out
that we had scarcely begun to collect contributions for

the capsule. I asked him if he would like to write a 'letter to the future', and said that I would speak to the Headmaster about when he should dig the hole. He then told me a very dubious joke about a man who had worked for McAlpine and went after a job as a grave-digger, in a town in the Midlands. To test his stamina he was asked to dig a trial grave and the supervisor said he would be back in a couple of hours to see how he was getting on. Apparently graves are in layers. By the time the supervisor returned our hero, accustomed to digging trenches, had gone down through two layers and bones were flying everywhere.

Jason assured me that this is true.

Friday 24.8.90

At which point the phone rang and this time it *was* Evelyn. It was. It was.

No way am I going to write down what we said.

Private!

KEEP OUT!!!!!!!

They're coming back earlier than expected, next week, but going straight up to Scotland (to slaughter grouse, probably. Only kidding!). Her father has something to do with somebody who works in Kuwait and she was saying how relieved they all are that this guy had got out before the invasion. This is the first time I've spoken to anyone who's even *thought* about it, I'll swear. At least they haven't got relatives out there. On the News last night there was a terrible video of the Iraqi President being *genial* with some of the British families in Baghdad. It was grisly. He reminded me of old cartoons of Stalin being Jolly Uncle Joe.

Eve rang up while I was still writing down my chat with Gerry. I must say I thought it was funny, Lord Snooty and his pals burying their capsule for a hundred years and then finding it's going to come up again after eight. But Gerry ain't amused and the last thing he said was, 'Don't mention this to anyone.'

Perhaps he did bury a corpse.

Anyway, I promised to nip up there again today and ask the contractors about rescuing it. So after work I leapt on the bike and off up the ring road to school. Twice in one week! And it's the holidays.

Fortunately the Bandicoot has gone off to the sillies and the caretaker's on holiday. Mr Mason, his assistant, doesn't live on the campus so there was no brass about. But there was a lorry unloading sand and a lot more bricks have arrived since yesterday, bright pink, like smoked salmon.

I went looking for a foreman or something of the sort and found a couple of guys pissing themselves laughing over The Feelie, which was a bit of luck. Not the laughing – the fact that they had The Feelie in mind. The luck, I mean. Oh, shut up!

'What do you want?' says one of them. He was wearing, in a temperature of 30°, a blue suit and green wellies. Must be the architect.

I explained about the Time Capsule. They thought I was fooling around at first so I stopped treating them like fellow-humans and got very deferential and told them how my big brother had been in charge of burying it and that he wanted it retrieved before just anyone got at it.

It *could* be just anyone, too; it's not a local firm that's doing the work.

'Are you asking us to dig it up for you?' said the one who wasn't an architect. (Quite possibly neither is an architect.)

'No,' I said, 'what I want to know is, would you mind if *I* dig it up?'

'What, all by yourself?'

I hadn't thought of that because I do not intend to go down to a depth of 120 cm single-handed. The earth's probably like rock after eight years with that thing standing on it. The soil's mainly clay there.

Then the architect got suspicious and said, 'You aren't an archaeologist in disguise, are you?' but in the end they agreed that I could go ahead next week, after The Feelie had been moved. I'd get Geoff to help, only he's taken off with a friend, into the wide blue yonder.

To be honest I can't see why the idiots who buried it shouldn't be the ones to dig it up. I wonder who they were.

Yesterday Iraq ordered all Western embassies in Kuwait to close and clear out, deadline tonight. All day troops have been stationed outside our embassy, and the Americans', but everyone is staying put. On the News at 5.40 it said the deadline had been extended.

Mum's at the bureau most of the time. Dad watches the News but I can't get him to talk about it (or anything else, come to that). He must have had enough of war. He was four when WWII broke out and then he got sent to Suez on National Service. And then for the rest of his life, the Cold War. I wonder if he's ever felt safe?

I was just beginning to.

APRIL 10TH 1982 SATURDAY

The Task Force has been joined by the *Canberra*, a cruise liner, and a roll-on roll-off ferry, such as is currently used to cross the English Channel, carrying armoured vehicles. On Monday the 200 mile Maritime Exclusion Zone comes into force. It has now been extended to cover merchant vessels and aircraft. The Defence Secretary says that the Navy will shoot to sink.

It occurs to me, after mentioning the Channel ferry, that by now you will certainly have a tunnel beneath the Channel. I believe the idea first occurred to Napoleon, for purposes of conquest, and no doubt the Vikings might have wished for one and the Romans before them. Even so, if the Channel ferries are no more, I dare say there are still small boats plying their trade across your rivers.

I went into town this morning to return some overdue library books for my mother who appears to be taking an inexplicable interest in business studies, and afterwards went to the reference library to see if there were any books worth buying. The library operates a scheme whereby members of the public may purchase books that have been withdrawn from stock. Many are in excellent condition. It was while I was perusing the shelves that I noticed Jo-Ann Rugg seated at one of the tables, pretending to read a periodical. I say 'pretending' because the periodical in question was *The Economist*, and Jo-Ann has no interest at all, as far as I know, in economics, although given my mother's volumes on business studies it may be that there has

been a sudden outbreak of feminism among the local
ladies! Naturally I went over to speak to her. She
seemed agitated and not over-pleased to see me. I
observed at once that she had been crying. It was
useless to pretend that I had not noticed so I asked if she
were feeling unwell.

She said, 'Oh shit, I came in here for a bit of peace but
it seems nowhere's safe.'

I could understand that because Jo-Ann's family is
numerous – she is the third eldest of seven – and very
noisy, particularly her father who has a reputation for
violence. He has twice been jailed for assault. On the
other hand a noisy family is not necessarily a cause for
tears. I apologized for disturbing her and asked if she
wanted to talk.

'You're the *last* person I could talk to,' she snapped.

I said that I had always thought we were friends. She
has often visited our house – in the company of others!

She began to cry again and apologized and said that
it wasn't my fault. People were beginning to look at us
so I suggested that we left and went somewhere for
coffee.

She agreed so we went to the Compass Rose Wine
Bar which is usually quite empty at that hour – as
indeed it proved to be. Jo-Ann recovered her
composure rapidly and became her usual lively self. I
asked her again what had been the matter, but she just
laughed and said it was something private and
probably she was worrying unnecessarily.

'It does help to talk things over with friends,' I said.

'Not this,' she said.

'It will all be the same in a hundred years,' I told her.
Rather trite, as no doubt you will agree, but of course

that phrase is on my mind, at the moment, on account of this diary.

You will probably have noted that the diary is becoming more personal.

This was not my original intention, but I feel it would be dishonest to avoid certain areas. After all, Jo-Ann and I and the others are the 'authors' of this Time Capsule. I suspect that our daily lives, unspectacular though they are, will be of as much interest to you as the global spectrum which, after all, will be very well documented. You will already know the outcome of the Falklands conflict, the Iran/Iraq war and all the other international concerns and upheavals of which I write. Perhaps you live under a Soviet-dominated regime, Britain being just part of the Eastern Block. But you will not have known that eighteen-year-old Jo-Ann Rugg was weeping in the reference section of the public library at 11 am on April 10th 1982. And even I don't know why.

Saturday 25.8.90

Amazing. Now the Gulf Crisis has been wiped off the headlines but not, incredibly, by something worse.

Yesterday evening there was a news flash, just after the ads in the middle of _Murder, She Wrote_ which Mum watches religiously when she's not working. When I saw the newsreader come on I thought, Oh God, what's happened? but it was good news. One of the Beirut hostages, an Irishman, has been released. They said he would be a couple of months ago but nothing came of it. Now he's actually out! He was interviewed on the News today, looking ill. He had word of some of the other hostages, too. I suppose it was important that he should be seen and heard but I should think that it was the last thing he felt like doing. And yesterday they showed his sisters being told he was free. It was like intruding on something private. It _was_ intruding on something private. It doesn't matter what happens to you these days, someone comes barging in and shoves a microphone up your nose, wanting to know how you feel.

I watched the News just now. Actually it looks as though nothing else has happened. The embassies are besieged but they haven't been invaded. Look what I just wrote – _nothing else has happened._ Of course it hasn't, anywhere, in the entire world. Nothing has happened.

I've been feeling really lousy today. It came on last night which is why I was watching telly with the old folks at home instead of whooping it up down the Corn Exchange like most Friday nights. And I knocked off work today at lunchtime instead of 5.30. I usually stay at Chandler's all day Saturdays. I haven't felt this bad for years.

Early night.

The UN says sanctions can be enforced with force. How else do you *enforce* something – with a bright smile and a feather duster?

APRIL 11TH 1982 EASTER SUNDAY

Large numbers of relatives converged upon the house to join us for Easter lunch. I wonder, does England still have an Established Church and religious holidays? Is Easter still celebrated, and Christmas? And if so, have they become entirely secular festivals? Already there must be more practising Muslims in this country than there are Christians.

I can hardly claim that we celebrate Easter as a religious festival but we still exchange Easter eggs, mainly for the benefit of the children. This year *they* secretly prepared an Easter egg hunt for *us*, with rather obvious clues concealed around the garden. Of course we made heavy weather of solving them, which fooled (and delighted) Geoffrey. Hugh is more sceptical and knew perfectly well that we were only pretending to be puzzled! I imagine that his long periods of illness in childhood have made him unusually contemplative (and hence observant) for his age – almost nine. He has been in good health now since January, his last major attack, but August and September are dangerous months for him on account of the harvest dust. Today however he was running about and shouting with his cousins (my mother's sister's children).

While we were having lunch the telephone rang. Hugh went to answer it as he was nearest to the door, but came back immediately and said that whoever it was had hung up when he answered.

My mother said, 'That is the fifth time this week. Is it one of your friends fooling around, Gerry?'

I replied that my friends do not go in for this kind of thing.

My father said, 'When are the calls made?' and my mother said it was usually in the evenings.

'Well, let me answer the phone for the next few days,' my father said.

'What difference will that make?' my mother said.

'They might get discouraged if they hear a man's voice.'

'Cowed, you mean?' said my Aunt Susan.

'There are men who entertain themselves by terrorizing women over the telephone,' my father said. He and Susan are not good friends.

'I'm not terrorized,' said my mother, 'just irritated. Whoever it is has had me out of the bath twice.'

'Then let me answer it,' said my father.

'I'd have let you answer it when I was in the bath,' said my mother, 'only you were out.'

This may strike you as very quaint. It is quite possible that by now (2082) people will have portable telephones beside them in the bathroom, garden, etc. Perhaps you will even have televisual phones, showing a picture of the caller. As yet, I believe, this remains within the realm of science fiction.

All the same, it is unsettling to know that someone is taunting us in this manner. On one of the occasions my mother mentioned, it was I who answered the phone, but thought nothing of it, assuming that it was a wrong number.

At least they are not obscene calls, in which an anonymous caller, usually, one supposes, male, makes sexually suggestive propositions to the recipient, usually female.

Do you still have those?

Sunday 26.8.90
Ill.

APRIL 12TH 1982 EASTER MONDAY

The Exclusion Zone came into force at 4 am today and the EEC has finally united in agreeing to ban all Argentinian imports.

There was a curious article in the paper this morning entitled 'The Laws of War'. One sentence caught my eye because it answered a question that I have been asking myself for a long time: 'Are we at war?' I have heard, of course, recordings of Neville Chamberlain declaring war on Germany in 1939 and it struck me recently that we do not seem to have declared war on Argentina. The sentence I noticed said, 'War does not have to be formally declared to bring the laws of war into force.'

I can't say that I have ever thought about war having laws. I cannot tell if the term 'Geneva Convention' means anything to you, but in our time we frequently hear it mentioned. Like so many things one is accustomed to, one never thinks very deeply about it, but seeing the word 'Geneva' mentioned further on in the article, I read the rest of it.

'It is a basic principle of the laws of war that even states guilty of unprovoked aggression have exactly the same rights and duties as other belligerents.'

(From the 1907 Hague Regulations) 'The attack or bombardment, by whatever means, of towns, villages, dwellings or buildings, which are undefended, is prohibited.'

The 1925 'Geneva Protocol' prohibits the use in war of asphyxiating, poisonous or other gases.

'Hospital ships, at least if their presence is formally

notified ten days in advance, may not be attacked or captured.'

There was a Genocide Convention in 1948.

Pillage is prohibited.

Certain words stand out: 'principle'; 'guilty'; 'rights'; 'duties'; 'prohibited'; 'notified . . . in advance'.

It reads like a notice from the local council – as if you couldn't go to war without filling out forms in triplicate, getting your signature witnessed by the bank manager and sending them in not less than six weeks before you intend to begin.

It's incredible to think that people draw up rules for warfare and call them *laws* – which can be broken. They might as well announce that war has been made illegal, while they're about it, but then, by the time you read this, war *may* have been made illegal.

Do you realize what an act of faith this diary is? I must tell you that at this moment few of us really believe that there will be anybody left to read it in a hundred years.

I've just remembered that Greg Rugg, Jo-Ann's eldest brother, is in the army. She rarely mentions him but it occurs to me that it may be him that she is worrying about. I don't know where he's stationed or even what he does but I suppose he could be sent to the South Atlantic.

Monday 27.8.90

Yesterday's paper: The leaders of Britain's one million Muslims object to the economic blockade of Iraq.

Today's paper: GULF CRISIS BACK FROM THE BRINK. Haven't I seen that somewhere before?

On the News the main story was the verdict in a very long fraud trial. Everything seems to have gone off the boil while I had my day out.

I haven't been that ill for years. I'd forgotten what the signs were. I spent yesterday in bed and most of today. Flat out.

Even writing this is tiring.

The Salbutamol didn't help much but it's so long since I used it it's probably way past its best-before date. It took Mum half an hour to find it.

Gerry rang last night. Couldn't get up to speak to him. Asked Dad to take a message but he said he'd ring again. Must have been about the capsule. Why couldn't he tell Dad? What's the fuss anyway? Fortunately Dad doesn't think to ask me what's going on. Doesn't care anyway.

Geoff brought me a chocolate orange to cheer me up. That was nice of him. Trouble is, chocolate makes me wheeze. He'd forgotten that.

So'd I – till I'd started it.

Phone.

If that's Gerry, tell him I'll ring tomorrow.

Tell him I'm dead.

APRIL 13TH 1982 TUESDAY

Something rather unsettling has happened. I was alone in the house this evening, except for the children who had gone to bed. At half past nine the phone rang. Usually when I answer our phone I give the number first of all: Calderley 703514 – I wonder who has it now, if such things as phone numbers still exist – but remembering what had been going on lately I just picked up the receiver and said hello. I don't think I sound much like my father but a woman's voice said, 'Tony?' I said, 'No, this is Gerald, can I take a message?' and then there was a long pause and the voice said, 'Oh!' then, 'I'm sorry, I must have a wrong number,' and the line went dead. Of course, it may very well have been a wrong number, but my father is known as Tony. And most people who find they have dialled a wrong number sound annoyed or disappointed, but not alarmed.

In the South Atlantic the Naval Blockade (Exclusion Zone) is now in effect. The Argentinian warships so far remain in port and our submarines are lying in wait. The Argentinians are trying to persuade the EEC to lift its trade embargo. Alexander Haig has been at Downing Street. The talks on ending the crisis have foundered.

An item in the newspaper today revealed that black families live in fear on council estates. There are very few black families living locally so the problem does not arise, as far as I know, but I've been thinking of Jo-Ann's circumstances. The estate where she lives is very run-down and I should not care to go there at night, alone. You might like to read a description of our local estate. It is called Meadowlands and comprises mainly low-level housing within four six-storey blocks of flats and a shopping precinct. Jo-Ann's family live in Windrush House, on the fifth floor. I should not care to live on the fourth! I wonder if the estate is still there, and if so, what has become of it. The policy of the present Conservative administration is for council tenants to purchase their houses (as part of the drive towards privatization in this country) although there does not seem to have been much of a move in this direction in Meadowlands. A few of the terraced and semi-detached houses are sporting double glazing and Texas doors, but they are in the minority. A Texas door, by the way, takes its name from a do-it-yourself chain. The most popular model has a fanlight built into it which can look very strange when fitted into a doorframe that already has a fanlight *above* it. Perhaps such doors are now prized as specimens of late twentieth-century architecture!

This afternoon I took delivery of the first contributions for the Time Capsule. If you have already looked through them you will see what I meant about Adam Ant. You may have already played the record. The donor assures me that 'The Human League' will be a name that resounds down the ages. William Porter, of the Upper Sixth, has made a videotape in response to a suggestion made to him by Tim Finch after our inaugural committee meeting. It is entitled *A Day in the Life of Calderley*. Apparently he borrowed his uncle's video camera and last Monday spent a whole day filming in town from dawn to nightfall. I haven't had a chance to look at it yet – perhaps tomorrow morning – but he said he thought

the effect was *ciné vérité*, that is, hand-held, as he did
much of the filming while riding his bicycle.

My parents came home just now. My father asked if
there had been any phone calls. I said only a message
for Mum which was on the pad, and a wrong number.
I have been thinking about that wrong number. I have
a feeling I recognized the voice.

Tuesday 28.8.90

Back to normal, I think. Don't feel a lot like digging holes.

Went to health centre before work and got a new prescription – just in case. Wondered if the flowers would get up my nose, but OK so far.

When I got home Mum had left a note by the phone. Gerry had rung. Would I ring him?

Well, I did. I'd have thought he'd be at work but he said he had the day off. And he said, had I done anything yet about Thrust 15? 'Yes,' I said, 'I'd be doing something right now if I hadn't been ringing you. I'm going up to school after lunch.'

'What's the delay?' he said, sounding really apprehensive. Delay???

'Look,' I said, 'they aren't moving the thing till today. For all I know they haven't moved it yet. What's the rush?' I said.

He was very quiet. I thought the line had been cut. Then he said, 'Has anyone else said anything about it?' I assumed he meant The Feelie so I told him what the teachers call it. He said, 'No, not the sculpture, the Time Capsule.' I said, 'Who else knew about it, then?'

'Quite a lot of us,' he said and went quiet again.

'Like, the whole school?'

'There were ten of us on the committee,' he said, 'and about thirty-five in the Upper Sixth. Not everyone contributed, but a lot did.'

'You mean, they might all turn up and start digging?'

'No,' he said, getting riled again. I wasn't taking him seriously enough. Well, I never have. No one could

take our Gerald as seriously as he takes himself. 'I don't
want just anybody digging it up.'

I asked him if he minded Geoff giving me a hand, if
Geoff shows up in time.

'Is that strictly necessary?' he asked and then he asked
if I'd told Geoff anything. When I said I hadn't he said
good, he'd rather I kept it to myself.

I explained that I'd just had an asthma attack and
didn't want to tax my failing strength, etc.

He said he was sorry about that and said he hadn't
realized I'd started getting attacks again. (Neither had I
and I'm keeping my fingers crossed that it was a one-
off.) He said he wouldn't have involved me at all, only
there was no one else available.

'See how it goes,' he said. 'If you have trouble get
Geoff to help you – but look, do try to keep quiet
about this, won't you? Don't tell *anyone*.'

I said that I'd had to tell the contractors and he said
are they local? He seemed very relieved when I said that
they weren't.

What the hell is going on? What *has* he got buried
down there?

Anyway, I went up to school after lunch and The
Feelie's still there. The crane hasn't arrived. Long may
it continue to do so. Not arrive, I mean.

On the international front Saddam Hussein has said
that all women and children are free to leave Iraq.
Don't know whether anyone believes him or not. The
arms build-up goes on but no one does anything but
talk. Is this a good thing or is it just giving everybody
time to get on a war footing?

The defendants in the fraud trial I mentioned
received prison sentences. Some people, Dad included,

think this is unnecessarily harsh. He said you can get sentenced to less than that for killing someone. I bet no one would think it harsh if they'd actually gone out and *stolen* the money.

A policeman has been shot dead – while investigating a car theft. There wasn't a riot or a bank raid; he wasn't even arresting anyone. He was just shot – because he was there.

APRIL 14TH 1982 WEDNESDAY

This morning I watched William Porter's video. I can see what he means by *ciné vérité*, as in many shots the camera is the most active thing in operation. 'Ducking and weaving' is the best description. I rang William to ask if he didn't think some editing might be advisable but he said that he didn't have the facilities and anyway, the whole point of the video was to show what the town was like in 1982, what kind of transport we have, what sort of clothes we wear and so on: all the things that are sure to change in the future, and this was why he had spent so much footage just filming streets. For a start, he said, the Restmore factory is almost certain to come down because it occupies a prime site for development (the junction of Union Street and Warwick Road). To be honest, the most exciting scene is two men, one of them Mr Rugg, having a violent argument outside Laura Ashley. If you haven't seen it yet, this incident occurs about five minutes from the beginning. You may not realize how incongruous it is. Laura Ashley is (was?) a chain of shops specializing in extremely traditional clothes for women. Neither of the combatants seems to be the type who would purchase anything in there. Mr Rugg certainly isn't. I pointed out to William that he had better not mention his video to anyone else or the rest of the class might want to see it and Jo-Ann might not care to have her father's belligerent tendencies preserved for posterity.

'Funny you should say that,' said William. 'Jo-Ann's in it, too.'

I hadn't noticed and asked him where she appeared.

'Find out for yourself,' he said and hung up, laughing. I started to watch the video again using the pause button to examine it more closely, but it is a time-consuming business and I have a great deal of school work to do. I'll try again later.

Haig is flying to Washington with fresh ideas for peaceful negotiation. Our Parliament is said to be hopeful of success. Argentina is pessimistic. Our Navy has requisitioned another five ships.

When I began this diary the Falklands conflict was, as you might say, 'a cloud on the horizon no bigger than a man's hand', and in my international report I gave precedence to the war between Iran and Iraq. Saddam Hussein says he is ready to withdraw his troops from Iranian soil if he has guarantees that Iran would not invade Iraqi-owned territory.

There was a 'quip' in the paper today which I must say I found rather apposite. It said that Haig's breakfast date had burst his time capsule as he has now crossed fourteen time zones in four days!

There were no phone calls this evening.

Wednesday 29.8.90

'War is cruelty and you cannot refine it.' William T. Sherman. He was the one who also said, 'War is hell'. That didn't stop him waging it, though. Still, I can see what he means. Warfare is so vile that it is ridiculous to try and clean it up, passing resolutions not to use particular kinds of weapons and so on.

On the other hand, Cardinal Newman (who was never a soldier) wrote: 'There is such a thing as legitimate warfare: war has its laws; there are things that may fairly be done, and things which may not be done . . . '

I think I go along with Sherman. I seem to remember that he liked to get things over with quickly, to save wasting lives in the future, which was more or less the excuse made for dropping the Atom Bombs on Japan in 1945. Do I go along with *that*?

It looks as if S. Hussein really will let the women and children go. At the moment, though, there is more talk about the sentences passed in the Guinness trial than there is about the Gulf. We've just sent four more ships out there and Neil Kinnock has requested that Parliament be recalled.

That's incredible. Could we actually go to war while Parliament is in recess? I mean, all these politicians on holiday, George Bush playing golf, and over there people are taken hostage, men are starving in the desert, refugees are pouring into Jordan. But Parliament's on holiday and I'm selling flowers.

I went up to school on the way home from work. The Feelie is still there and it doesn't look like anyone's been doing anything for the last week. That is, it looks like your average building site.

I know what's going to happen. They'll get started the day we go back to school and we'll have pneumatic drills and pile drivers and concrete mixers under the windows for a couple of terms. Plus ghetto blasters.

Well, blast my ghetto! (A useful oath.)

Tomorrow I can ring Evelyn.

Stop press: The case of the Birmingham Six is going to the Court of Appeal again. The last time was in 1987. They were convicted in 1974 of killing twenty-one people in a pub bombing. Suppose they were innocent all along, like the Guildford Four. It doesn't bear thinking about.

APRIL 15TH 1982 THURSDAY

This morning Naseem Amin came round. Geoffrey let her in. He said, 'There's an Indian lady to see you,' which surprised me, but I wasn't much less surprised when I saw who it was. Naseem is Pakistani, not Indian, and a Muslim. Although we are all very friendly at school she does not socialize with us. She said, 'I have got something for you to put in the Time Capsule.'

I said, 'What is it?'

She gave me an envelope and said, 'It's a death threat.'

I thought she was joking and said, 'Who are you threatening?'

Naseem said, 'Don't be stupid. I am giving this to you for two reasons. One, you will be the person who seals the capsule and two, because you have no sense of humour.'

I thought she was having trouble with her English. She is a brilliant mathematician but is re-sitting Language O-level. 'Do you mean I am serious?'

'If you like,' she said, 'but what I meant was that if I trust you with this you will not make light of it and tell other people.' I wasn't quite sure if she'd said what she meant but I got the drift of it.

'Where did you get it from?' I said.

'It was sent to my father,' she said, 'to warn him what would happen if he went to the police again about the people who come into our shop.' Mr and Mrs Amin run a kind of delicatessen/off licence, the latter a shop where beers, wines and spirits may be purchased outside public house licensing hours.

I said, 'Which people?'

Naseem said, 'At night there are certain people who come to the shop and take things, mainly drink, without paying. My father has been attacked, we find things sprayed on the shop front in the mornings, windows become broken. We went to the police once before, but they said we must have witnesses. They said there was no racial motive, it was just vandalism.'

I was reading the death threat by this time. It was addressed to 'You fat Paki bastard'.

'That Time Capsule,' said Naseem, 'it is supposed to be a picture of this town in 1982. I am part of this town. Who else is going to tell the future what it was like to be an Asian in Calderley in 1982? Lucy Ashton? You will all say like it does in the paper: "This town is proud of its race relations record," because we have an empty garage for a mosque.'

I said, 'Naseem, I thought we are all friends.'

She said, 'Yes, we are – not all of us, but most – but you do not *know*. What you write in that diary about 1982, it doesn't say anything like this, does it?'

I said, 'Why did you mention Lucy?'

Then she told me.

If you haven't found it yet, the death threat issued to Mr Habib Amin is in the Jiffy Bag (that brown padded envelope) sealed with insulating tape.

When I began this diary I decided that on the day before we close the capsule I would let everyone read it, but looking at what I have just written about my conversation with Naseem, I begin to see that I can't possibly let anyone else read it, not only because of what Naseem told me but, now I come to think of it, because of all the personal observations I have made.

As I shall seal the capsule, as Naseem pointed out, I
alone shall be ultimately responsible for what goes into
it. I promised her that the death threat would go in and
I might as well add that she is quite certain that the
person who wrote it is Lucy's brother Simon. He is the
worst of their persecutors.

Naseem said something terrible to me as she left. 'We
cannot hope for justice now, I am resigned to that, but
one day I want people to know what it was like for my
family in this quiet little town with its good race
relations record.'

She is willing to wait for a hundred years. She made
me swear not to tell anyone about this, because of what
might happen to her father if word gets out.

Mrs Thatcher says that if the Maritime Exclusion
Zone is breached 'We shall then take the necessary
action – let no one doubt that.'

Thursday 30.8.90

Just now *another* call from Gerry. This time I came straight out with it.

'What's with this bleeding capsule?' I said. 'Are you sure it's a Time Capsule and not a time *bomb*?'

He answered me very levelly. I never really thought before about what that actually means, but I could hear him deliberately keeping his voice steady.

'I told you,' he said, 'when we buried that capsule we intended it to stay there for a hundred years. It's not so ridiculous. There are Time Capsules concealed under all sorts of things, Cleopatra's Needle, for instance. It's not funny!'

I hadn't meant to laugh. Well, I hadn't meant to let him hear me, but it just struck me that our Feelie isn't in the same league as Cleopatra's Needle. He went on about how some people might have been very frank about, well, other people, and if the things they'd written got into circulation it might cause a lot of ill-feeling.

Sounds highly suspicious to me. I'm sure he's got a body down there. I wonder if there were any murders committed at the time – I asked him very casually exactly *when* it was buried and he said May 4th 1982. That must have been around the time of the Falklands. Funny, I was thinking about that a couple of weeks ago, wasn't I?

Maybe someone concealed a murder weapon in the capsule, a bloodstained hatchet with tell-tale hairs on it . . . Do fingerprints ever fade, I wonder? I'm going to have a great time going through this capsule when I get it, I can tell you. I *can* tell you, can't I?

Can't tell anyone else. Gerry wants me to keep shtumm.

The Feelie hasn't shifted yet.

Neither have the hostages in Iraq.

Eight o'clock, time to ring Eve. For the last time in Boston. She'll be in Aberdeen by Saturday night.

APRIL 16TH 1982 FRIDAY

It looks as if we are in for a long naval blockade. The Government no longer expects Haig's mission to Buenos Aires to be successful and General Galtieri has reaffirmed his determination to defend the Argentinian conquest of 'Las Malvinas'. Large numbers of Argentinian warships are reported to be setting sail.

Last October President Sadat of Egypt was assassinated. Yesterday his five killers were executed. I wonder if capital punishment has been restored in your time. As you probably know, it was abolished in the UK in 1969 but there are frequent demands for its return, for terrorist offences especially, and the murder of policemen. Last term we had a sixth form debate about this. The voting was heavily in favour of restoring capital punishment to the statute book. 'The Motion was carried,' as we say. I seconded it.

I have been reading Naseem's death threat again. If it had been received by my father he would have taken it straight to the police and it is appalling to think that the Amins feel this, for them, would do more harm than good. On the other hand, I imagine the sender would be very hard to trace. It has been written on a word processor, a machine which we consider to be 'state of the art' but which may strike you as antiquated – as indeed it must be. In detective novels writers of anonymous letters are always traced because of defects on the typeface of their typewriters, an update of recognizable traits in handwriting. But this doesn't seem to apply to word processors.

I wonder how long all this has been going on. As I

said, Naseem has always been on friendly terms with
all of us and I suppose I've always assumed that she has
a close friend among the girls, but from what she told
me yesterday, apparently not. And she has only
confided in me because of the capsule.

Friday 31.8.90

September tomorrow. Back to school in four days. Where has this holiday _gone_?

Came home via school with _extreme reluctance_. I'm getting sick of making that trip in the holidays and it adds about two miles to the journey, but it paid off at last. When I arrived I thought I was witnessing a public hanging. From the road I saw what looked like a gibbet with a corpse dangling from it and slowly turning in the wind, but as I came up the drive I saw it was the jib of a crane mounted on the back of a lorry, and The Feelie, wrapped in sacking, was hanging from a hook. (Jib – gibbet: any connection?)

The slab was still there, though. I'd thought it was joined to the feet of the The Feelie – its wrist, actually.

One of the workmen who was standing around, workmanlike, said, 'Oi, clear off. No unauthorized personnel on site,' but I explained that I had permission and told him why. He wasn't very pleased. What would happen, he wanted to know, if I started squirreling under that slab and it caved in on top of me? I said I'd rather hoped the slab would be going too.

'Well, it will,' he said, 'but I don't know when.'

'Couldn't it go now?' I said. I explained that school would begin again in a few days and I wanted to get this out of the way before crowds started gathering. He went and had a word with someone and it turned out that the slab was due to be moved as well. I could do any excavating work over the weekend, he said, when there was no one around to be responsible. At least, I think that's what he was driving at.

Saturday's out. It'll have to be Sunday.

Of course, this now means that at least four people on the site know about the Time Capsule.

I can't help that. There'd be hell to pay if I just started digging.

In Iraq they're all at the airport, but nothing's happened yet.

APRIL 17TH 1982 SATURDAY

I've been having another look at William Porter's video. There are some very odd things about it, notably the weather. I don't recall what the weather was actually like that day but it seems to have changed dramatically around mid-morning. In the early shots, up to just after the fight outside Laura Ashley, the skies are overcast and the pavements wet. Then it is suddenly dry and sunny. Still, the early shots appear to be *very* early. There is hardly anyone about and in the fight scene I have just noticed that the shops are still shut so it must have been before 9 am. It took me a long while to spot Jo-Ann – near the beginning – going into the health centre in Warwick Road. I hope you will make allowances for the fact that the quality of an amateur videotape differs widely from that of a commercial production. You may even be wondering how I can have recognized anyone!

This evening we have a committee meeting at Lucy's house. I wonder about how I shall feel, going there after what Naseem told me. And how will Naseem feel?

General Galtieri has offered to share rule in the Falklands up till the end of the year, while sovereignty is negotiated. Britain responds by insisting that at least some of the Argentinian troops be withdrawn. Javier Perez de Cuellar (the new Secretary General of the United Nations) has begun preparations for a possible request to have the Falklands administered by the UN. I have been blithely referring to the UN throughout this chronicle, on the assumption that it will still exist in your time. I suspect in fact that it will either have been superseded or become redundant, for one reason or another. Or it may even have become united!

In the Gulf it is believed that the downfall of President Saddam Hussein is not simply inevitable but imminent. To whose advantage, I wonder?

11.30 pm. In a way the meeting was a success. People have accumulated a number of contributions for the Time Capsule. Will Thomson has made two tapes of radio programmes from all four BBC stations and one or two commercial channels. We have also been given a bundle of photographs and some of the 'ephemera' I mentioned earlier – bus tickets, rail timetables, a programme for a concert given by one 'Captain Sensible', a fly poster for a protest meeting (protesting against the Task Force) and some beer mats, these last being used as 'coasters' under glasses in public houses. Many people collect them. William Sargent has collected together a bundle of advertisements clipped from newspapers and magazines for various 'consumer goods'. I have not yet decided which of these items I shall ultimately include, but the advertisements will certainly be among them. They may have already afforded you some amusement!

On the way to Lucy's house I met Tim Finch who was coming to the committee meeting, walking with William Porter, who was not! William said, 'Did you spot Jo-Ann yet?'

I said yes, down Warwick Road and he said that he hadn't noticed that one. He'd been thinking of the shot outside the town hall. I shall have to investigate this further. I asked him about the sudden changes in the weather and he confessed that he'd *begun* to film on Saturday but the light had been so bad that he had packed it up and resumed at the same hour on Monday. That explains it.

Jo-Ann was not there this evening. Nor was Mark Lovell. None of us has seen him since the end of term. Naseem sent her apologies. Simon Ashton was the one who let Tim and me in when we arrived. He seems very pleasant.

He *seems* very pleasant.

Saturday 1.9.90

I just caught the end of the News and it said the first planes of the Baghdad Airlift had just taken off.

I rang Gerry last night and told him that the Calderley Earthlift would begin on Sunday. That is, I told his girlfriend or fiancée, or whatever she is. Antoinette. He was out.

She doesn't sound very clued up. 'What is Time Capsule?' she said. Perhaps they don't go in for that kind of thing over there. I'm surprised we do, to tell you the truth. It seems more like the kind of thing Americans would do. They're much more interested in history than we are. All we seem to care about is heritage which is history with the unsaleable bits taken out. Watered down for public consumption.

It isn't at all like Gerry to be so frantic about *anything*. All those phone calls. He goes for weeks without getting in touch. Months. I don't think he even remembers we're here, half the time. He forgot my birthday, didn't he? Curses! If I hadn't reminded him I wouldn't be stuck with all this garbage. I don't even think he trusts me all that much, I just happen to be the man on the spot. A pity some of his old mates aren't on the spot, too.

On the way home from work I went and had a look at the site. I was surprised how much they'd done. The slab – plinth – was in the middle of the rose bed and The Feelie was back on the plinth only now it is facing the other way. It used to point in the direction of the staffroom but the way it's been set up it looks as if it's groping towards the gate, though you can't see the gate from there because of the evergreen hedge that shields the eyes of the Bandicoot from the sight of the vulgar herd flooding in from Foundry Hill every morning at 8.45.

He's probably back from the sillies by now. Everyone must be back from wherever they went. I'd be having tearful reunions if it weren't for Gerry and his box of tricks. The only friend I've seen for weeks is Dan Campion and that's because he lives in the next street. I suppose I kind of lost touch with people when I took up with Eve.

The caretaker's back too. I saw him out in his garden prowling up and down the Brussels sprouts. He saw me and greeted me in his usual genial fashion, 'What the hell do you think you're doing,' etc. etc. so over I trot to tell him what's going on. Deep suspicion – he distrusts all 580 of us, but I've always got on OK with him because his wife used to teach at the same school as Mum, way back when, before I was born. There was her and Mum and Barbara. They've all kept in touch.

After I'd explained, he came over to have a look at where I was going to dig. The patch of earth where the slab was is about the size of a grave (very suitable, if you think about it) and very solid-looking.

'Lend you a pick-axe if you like,' Mr Whiting said. I hadn't been thinking in terms of pick-axes, but it ought to save time.

Still, *five* people know.

APRIL 18TH 1982 SUNDAY

I once saw a very old film from the 1960s called *Blow-up*, in which a photographer realizes that he may unwittingly have recorded a murder in a park during a modelling session. He doesn't suspect anything until someone comes round and tries to get hold of his film. Then he blows up every frame, larger and larger, until he can see, in the bushes, a hand holding a gun.

Nothing like that has happened with William's video, fortunately, but I spent the whole morning examining it and quite a little drama is unfolding. That sounds appallingly flippant in view of what I think I have uncovered. Or rather, William has uncovered. I found Jo-Ann's other appearance. She is standing, as William said, outside the Town Hall, apparently waiting for a bus, but she is looking fixedly in one direction, to the left, and just in frame, for a second, is someone walking towards her. It looks to me like Mark Lovell. You can't see his face but I recognize his coat. It is an old RAF greatcoat and I was with him when he bought it last year, in 'Second Time Around' on the Parade. When I'd seen that I back-tracked to the famous fight outside Laura Ashley, because the 'man' scuffling with Mr Rugg is wearing an RAF greatcoat. Now all this happened on Saturday morning (April 3rd) when Mark was supposed to be ill with a virus. I don't think William noticed any of this. Judging by the condition of the video he was too worried about staying on his bike, which is probably why he didn't notice Jo-Ann where *I* noticed her. In that scene he is actually filming two women in saris, with umbrellas, hurrying across the road in the wind. It's a lovely shot, it's so pretty, but on the edge of the frame is Jo-Ann, going into the side gate of the Health Centre. She's only there for a second. I recognize the gate, too. It is the one that leads to the ante-natal clinic. I went there with my mother once or twice, when she was expecting Hugh.

I shouldn't be writing any of this down. The diary was never intended to be a personal record, an intrusion into other people's lives, any more than William's video was. Moreover, I don't think *he* has any idea of what he filmed. I don't know what I shall do if the others ask to see it – create a diversion, perhaps, at crucial moments.

I hope you who are reading this can sympathize with my predicament.

The photographs I was given are entirely innocuous, of people's houses, pets, parents, motor bikes. I confess I looked at them all with a magnifying glass, but there is nothing peculiar in any of them.

Term begins tomorrow. This evening I telephoned Mark Lovell. There was no one at home.

Sunday 2.9.90

Set out early. Nobody else was up. It's a good thing no one asks many questions in our house. Mr Whiting had left the pick-axe and a spade in his porch – he wasn't up, either. It was lovely up there, on Foundry Hill, in the early morning, a few pigeons cooing and the low sun shining through the trees. Yes, it was *that* early.

I stood there and *made* myself think of the Gulf. It didn't work. I mean, I could think of it, all right, but it wasn't spontaneous sympathy. I just can't keep all that in my head. I can't feel it. I tried telling myself that once upon a time I could have been sent out there. I might even have *wanted* to be sent out there, part of a fighting force. I'm seventeen. I could have been at Agincourt, Bosworth, Blenheim, Waterloo, the Somme. Kids lied about their age to get out and fight in the trenches – I mean *real* kids. In those days I would have seen old soldiers (say thirty years old) hacked about and mutilated, but I wouldn't have thought it could happen to me. It's only because of television that we all know now what happens when the shooting starts, and because of journalists who *won't* pretend that it's glorious and gallant and not really terribly dangerous. But even knowing doesn't make you *feel* what it would be like.

I remember at primary school doing a project on the London Blitz. We read about it and saw telly programmes about it, and an old lady who'd lived in the East End came and told us about it, but when we had to *write* about it, pretending we'd been there, I didn't know what to put. The teacher said, 'Use your imagination,' but I didn't have anything to imagine *with*. There was a university friend of Gerry's who came from Belfast. I asked him what it was like but he said that terrorist attacks were nothing like aerial bombardment. 'But what's it like when a bomb goes off?' I said, and he said he'd never actually seen it happen, close to.

Someone from Beirut would know, I suppose, or a Vietnamese, or a Cambodian. Barbara's ex-husband, Chris, fought in Vietnam. He was Australian.

I've noticed something rather nasty. Ever since the women hostages have started coming back from Baghdad the television has been referring to their husbands as 'menfolk'. It sounds like Wild West Frontier talk. Spurious. Incongruous. If we aren't careful it will happen to all of us, men and boyfolk.

Well, I dug all morning. At first I tried going down at the same rate over the whole area which is about two metres by just over one, but the soil is hard and clayey and caked. The pick-axe breaks it up but doesn't shift any. I've got to go down something like 120 cm and I don't know exactly where the damn thing is. Those film cases aren't very big.

When I went home for lunch I tried ringing Gerry again for more accurate information, such as, is it in the north west corner or in the middle? but there was no one at home, not even Antoinette. I was expecting him to ring me back after yesterday, but I don't imagine he has as much free time as I do – if he had I think he'd be over here himself, doing the digging. I'll give him the benefit of the doubt. Poor old Gerry. Come to think of it this is probably his problem. Not frantic, just frustrated.

Had a bright idea while looking out of the window.

Dad's been putting up a trellis half-way down the garden, using a post-hole borer. It's not a very big one but if I dig down to say 60 cm. I can then make a series of holes 20 cm apart which means I should get some idea of where it *isn't*.

I ought to have started all this sooner. I've only got tomorrow and Tuesday. I checked the calendar and it's the staff who go back on the 4th. We all start again on the 5th but I don't fancy scrabbling about in that hole with all the teachers peering at me out of the staffroom windows. The staffroom overlooks the quad. All today I've had the sensation of someone watching me from behind.

It was only The Feelie. Perhaps, slowly and unobserved, it is groping its way back to stand where it thinks it should be.

Anyway, I can make with the post-hole borer first thing tomorrow if I don't get an attack. I was feeling suspiciously breathless when I knocked off this evening.

'What have *you* been doing?' Mum said, giving me the hard look when I came in. I told her I'd been helping a friend on his allotment. I don't know why I lied – well, I couldn't tell her the truth, she'd have thought I was barmy, but it turned out I did the right thing. Anyway, she said, 'Huh! If you're that interested in digging there's plenty to do here.'

Gerry rang just as I was sinking into a well-deserved slumber in the bath. Such timing! Still, I might have drowned if he hadn't.

'Found it yet?' he said.

'Not quite,' I told him. I asked him how long it had taken him to dig the bloody hole in the first place. He said someone else had done that. Typical.

So I asked him very ironical, if there was a faint chance he knew where the capsule was in relation to the general layout.

One of those lo-o-o-o-o-o-ng silences.

'No.'

Big deal. I'm going to ache like crazy in the morning. It's started already.

Before he rang off he said again, 'I can trust you, can't I, Hugh?'

'I've started so I'll finish,' I said.

'I didn't mean that,' he said. 'I meant, you won't talk about this, to anyone.'

Omitting to mention the builders – and Mr Whiting – I said no, I wouldn't, but why not?

Dead serious, he was. 'It's far better that no one knows about this. You haven't told Mum and Dad?'

'Why, should they care?'

'They might be curious.'

Indifferent's nearer the mark. I don't think they care much what Geoff and I do so long as we don't get arrested.

'All right,' I said. 'I'll open it behind locked doors.'

'DON'T OPEN IT!' He nearly blew me across the room. He made me promise. I could hear him getting sweaty at the thought that if I'd been quicker off the mark with my excavation I might have opened it already.

Well, I won't, but . . .

Curiouser and curiouser.

APRIL 19TH 1982 MONDAY

Term begins – my last at school.

I saw Tim Finch and Bob Whiting talking with William Porter. None of them has seen Mark either, since the end of last term. Bob said that he heard he'd been staying with relatives.

I said to William, 'Didn't you see him when you were filming?'

William said, 'Should I have done?'

'You covered a lot of ground,' I said, but William said he couldn't recall it.

'I must have filmed hundreds of people without knowing it,' he said.

Well, I shan't say anything.

The sculpture has been delivered to the school. It is a remarkable work of art. Apparently it is one of a series of prototypes called 'Thrust'. The design we elected was No. 9. The sculpture is No 15 and, consequently, not quite what we expected. But it is very impressive, nonetheless.

Haig's talks in Buenos Aires have hit stalemate. Meanwhile the Vulcan bomber (you will find a photograph of that included) is being taken out of 'mothballs' (an antiquated method of protecting clothes in storage and here used figuratively) in order to take part in the recapture of the Falklands. Recently they were on sale for scrap at £3,000. Geoffrey was trying to persuade my father to buy one! A joke, of course. The twenty-nine marines and thirteen scientists (British) who were captured when South Georgia was first invaded are being flown home and not regarded as prisoners of war.

The Syrian Government has broken off all ties with Iraq in the Gulf. Islamic mediators will visit Iraq and Iran today to try to end the war. Will one end as another begins? Can there be anywhere in the world where there isn't a war at some time? What I meant to write there was: At any one time there seems to be a war somewhere in the world.

Monday 3.9.90

I've got it. Now what do I do with it?

In spite of being in mortal agony I got up at six and went straight to school. I shall only be working at Chandler's on Saturdays now that term's starting again. Mr Whiting had left the tools out on the porch for me and I had the post-hole borer. But it wasn't the post-hole borer that did the trick – not alone, that is. As I was toiling up Foundry Hill I was overtaken by Jason Ames on a superior machine.

He came straight to the point.

'What's all this about you digging up our Time Capsule?'

I told him I hadn't known it was anything to do with him.

'Not officially,' he said, 'but I dug the hole.'

Apparently he was grave-digging for the council back in 1982 and being an expert on holes, as you might say, lent a hand.

'There's a technique,' he said, 'like with anything else. Let's see what sort of a fist you've been making of it.'

It suddenly struck me that if this was all supposed to be a deadly secret it had got out bloody fast, so I asked him how he knew about it?

'Bob Whiting,' he said. 'He was on your brother's committee – you know about the committee?'

I didn't. Much.

'There were about ten of them, set themselves up to collect contributions for the capsule. Bob was one of them. He said his dad told him about your dig.'

Aaaaaaaaaagh! I hadn't the nerve to swear Mr Whiting to secrecy, it all sounded so childish. So, of course, he mentions it to the family. Bob works at the NatWest now, Wold Street branch. Dead respectable. I've never seen him knocking around with Jason, but then, I haven't been looking. It's amazing what you *don't* notice. (It strikes me, looking back, that Bob W. can't be very interested in the capsule or he'd have got it back himself, already.)

We'd arrived at the pit by now and Jason fell about laughing when he saw how I'd been chewing it up. These professionals, you know . . .

But he couldn't understand why I was digging it out at all. 'I'd have thought laying a patio over it would have made sure it stayed put,' he said.

I said I thought they were going to build a fifth form block.

'Yes, but this part will be paved,' he said. 'Haven't you seen the plans? They're in the Town Hall.'

They were in the school hall, too, but I never paid much attention to them.

'Gerry was afraid it would get dug up by accident,' I said, 'and fall into the wrong hands.'

'What, the rude uneducated proletariat?' he said. Gerry hadn't said that at all, in fact he's implied that's not what he's worried about, but I didn't want to give anything away. I just said that a JCB might mangle it if it went through the roof.

'JCB won't come anywhere near it,' Jason said. 'So, do you want to go on or leave it to be covered up again?'

I was very tempted to say leave it. Boy, was I tempted, but there is always a chance that it will

surface, whatever Jason thinks, impaled on the prong
of an earth-mover, and anyway, now that word is out
that it's on the move, someone else might start digging.
That's what seems to be bugging Gerry. I told Jason I'd
better get it back.

'OK,' said Jason. 'Well, you can leave this end for a
start. It's over here.'

The place he was pointing to was right on the edge
and *outside* of the place where the plinth had been. He
drew a square with his foot.

'Are you sure?' I said.

He said, 'Of course I'm sure. Look, you've been
digging where the slab was, haven't you. Well, did you
really think that come 2082 they were going to move a
damn great lump of rock so that a bunch of kids could
go rooting about under it? I dug *my* hole to one side so
it could be got at without disturbing the slab. I wasn't
chucked out of school for being thick,' he said.

I know what he was chucked out for. Everybody
does. He went to the CFE afterwards, but you have to
be a criminal lunatic to get slung out of that.

He had to go to work, then. I asked him if Gerry had
known about the alternative hole, intending to give
Number One Brother an earbashing for time-wasting,
muscle strain, etc., but he said no, probably not. By the
time the sculpture went up, he said, you couldn't see
where the hole had been because he'd smoothed it over.
(Come to think of it, he couldn't have known or he'd
have told me right away. Odd.)

So Jason went and I got digging, still spitting blood
over all the time and effort I'd wasted. I used the post-
hole borer as I'd meant to, once. I struck oil the very
first time. I did a couple more pokes to make sure I
hadn't hit a stone and then I really tore in.

I couldn't believe it when I found it. It was wrapped up in about six black plastic bin liners, but through the bin liners I could feel *chains*. I tore a hole through and had a look. The thing was chained and padlocked.

The chains turned out to be very useful . . . All I had to do was hook the pick under one of them and haul it out. Otherwise I'd have had to open up the hole round it. It wasn't heavy.

I filled in the hole and went home. Wheezing.

On the News it said that there is to be a nationwide survey of the country's two million asthma sufferers. 2,000 of us die every year. Just what I wanted to hear.

The airlift's been aborted.

APRIL 20TH 1982 TUESDAY

We've had another of those phone calls. My mother took it. She said that whoever it was didn't speak, just hung up, as usual. Later on, after my father came home, the phone rang again. This time he took the call. I was in my room and the door was open. I went to shut it, of course, and the first thing I heard him say was, 'Did you ring earlier?' And then, 'This has got to stop.' Then I shut the door. He was on the phone for about twenty minutes.

I am drawing the obvious conclusions. I have been trying to place the voice I heard that time I picked up the phone. Some friends of my parents, Chris and Barbara Paterson, used to visit us quite a lot, that is, they used to come to dinner and my parents went to their place. We all rented a holiday cottage in Somerset three years ago. The woman on the phone sounded very much like Barbara. She can't say her 'r's properly. Like 'Woy' Jenkins (an ex-Labour party politician, now with the Social Democratic Party). Geoffrey can mimic her very well and there used to be a certain amount of anxiety before they came in case he did it by accident while she was listening! Now I come to think of it, it must be about six months since we last saw them and they live only just the other side of Banbury.

Britain has ordered troop and ship reinforcements to head south. The Prime Minister has summoned her ministers to a 'war cabinet', saying that Argentinian peace proposals are unacceptable. Haig warns of a 'grave tragedy as time runs out'.

Looking at what I wrote above, I see I must

elucidate. We have two main political parties, Labour and Conservative, also the Liberals who have been in decline since the 1930s and the SDP, formed mainly by disaffected Labour politicians. It will be interesting to see how the electorate votes in the next General Election; more interesting than usual, that is.

10.45 pm. I have just done something of which I am very ashamed and which brought little consolation. While we were gathering to watch the ten o'clock News I went to the bookcase in the living room and got out a couple of our most recent photograph albums, and asked my mother if I could take one or two pictures for the Time Capsule.

'Don't take them out,' she said. 'Tell Tony [my father] which ones you want and he'll give you the negatives to get duplicate prints.'

This wasn't the reason at all. I started flipping through the pages, stopped at the ones with the snaps of our Somerset holiday and said, 'When are we going to see Chris and Barbara again? It's months since they were here.'

No one said anything at first. I looked round. Then my mother said, 'I see Barbara from time to time but I don't think . . . I mean, I think she and Chris have problems.'

She looked embarrassed, but only because she was telling me something personal about somebody else, I could see. My father didn't say anything at all.

Tuesday 4.9.90

It's in the shed. I'm in bed. Neil Kinnock made a
rousing speech at the TUC and promised *rights* not
favours. Labour's made a big comeback in the last few
months. If we have a General Election next year they
stand a good chance of getting in. Surely the Tories
won't get a *fourth* victory? There'll be no Falklands
factor this time. If Mrs Thatcher goes on and on and on
and on and on like she's always threatening, they *must*
be voted out, what with the Poll Tax, inflation,
education, unemployment, privatization, old Uncle
Tom Europe and all. It would be funny if I were to re-
read all this in ten years' time and she was *still* Prime
Minister. Reading it even in one year's time is going to
seem odd. Shall we have gone to war? Will it be over?
Suppose I buried *this* in a Time Capsule for a hundred
years. I can imagine people reading it and saying, 'Mrs
Thatcher? Saddam Hussein? Mikhail Gorbachev?
Arthur Scargill? The Guildford Four? The Birmingham
Six? Who *were* these guys?' Only historians will know.

Gerry rang up just now. Yes, I said, I'd got it, it was
safe, no I hadn't told Geoff or Mum or Dad. Then I
sprang my lovely surprise. 'Guess who helped me,
Gerald?'

I could hear him having a fit over the phone. 'Cool it,
Bro,' I said. 'He's a nice guy.'

'How did he know about it?'

I had to explain the Whiting connection, though I
made it very clear that Jason had known all about the
building plans all along. I also pointed out, between my
wheezing and his snorting, what I'd had to tell *Old*

Whiting and why, and that it hadn't occurred to me that he'd tell *Young* Whiting. I don't even know Young Whiting – not to speak to.

'Christ, he'll tell everybody,' said Gerald.

I can't think why he should, but even if he did, what's the hassle? Who is there left to tell, anyway? I am now on oath to guard the thing with my life.

I said, 'Why don't you come home and fetch it if it's that important?' but apparently he's in the States for three weeks. He was actually ringing, I *think*, from San Bernardino. He made it sound like he'd gone to Siberia. I wouldn't mind going to the States for three weeks, or even one week, but not right now, not now Eve's back. The place she's been staying in is so small I couldn't even find it on the map. Since she arrived back in Scotland we've rung each other every day. You didn't know that, did you? Haven't I been discreet?

Her school doesn't start again till next Monday. These private sector types . . .

Anyway, on the line to Brother Gerald I had one last go at finding out what is in the capsule.

'Look,' he said – as always – 'we've all changed a lot in eight years and people who put depositions [his very word] in that box didn't expect them to be seen in their lifetime. They acted in good faith. They trusted me. I owe it to them to protect their anonymity.'

Aha! Do I smell libel actions? What the hell could they all have been up to? Perhaps Gerry himself wrote something compromising. A declaration of undying love for Jason Ames, perhaps.

Aha! Wheeze. Wheeze.

Later. I've been thinking. (Yes folks! I can do that too. The all-singing, all-dancing, all-digging Hugh Marshall *thinks*. In glorious Technicolor.)

Shut up Marshall, this is serious.
Why doesn't he want Mum and Dad to know?
Mrs Whiting knows Mum.
Oh shit.

APRIL 21ST 1982 WEDNESDAY

If we lived in a bigger town I wonder if we should see so much of each other? I don't mean planned meetings, but the kind of accidental encounters that I am becoming so aware of. I am sure that it is the keeping of this diary that is making me so aware, rather, perhaps, as a newspaper reporter develops a 'nose' for a story. I've been looking back at the first few pages and thinking how misleading they might be. The murder which I recorded so avidly coincided with the absence from our committee meeting of Jo-Ann and Mark. Jo-Ann was subsequently worried that her parents might find out that she had not been with us. If this had been a bit of plotting in a novel it would look as if the two events were connected, but I only mentioned them because they concerned a) the diary as an account of daily life, and b) me as a friend of Jo-Ann. In fact thousands of other events took place which I neither knew about nor recorded. It looks as if the real connection was between Jo-Ann's absence and Mark's. There is also that fight on the Saturday morning between Jo-Ann's father and Mark. Mark is not at school. I rang him up last night but all I could get out of his mother was that he was away but would be back soon. As with another matter I am putting two and two together. Jo-Ann looks utterly miserable. I cannot say anything to anyone because I'm not supposed to know anything. I wish I were as unobservant as William Porter.

It is a great relief to be able to confide in these pages. The murder trail seems to have gone cold. In a way

I am sorry. I was rather looking forward to charting its progress up to the triumphal discovery of the murderer. Now it just looks like a red herring. I hope you haven't been disappointed.

The Fleet is now only days away from the Falklands and it is reported, by the Americans, that a fast destroyer squadron has been detached from the Task Force and may reach South Georgia in less than 48 hours. Last night the Cabinet took only an hour to endorse a continued search for a negotiated settlement but, as I have just indicated, time is running out.

I have conferred with the others about getting Jason Ames to dig the hole for the Time Capsule. The consensus was that we are in favour as we are all now very short of time, with examinations looming. Robert Whiting said that in his opinion the less said about this to the Headmaster the better. On the other hand, he said, his old man (who is the caretaker) would not give a damn either way, so we should arrange for Jason to come and dig on a Sunday – about the only day the Head stays away from the place, apparently. 'You can't imagine how inhibiting it is to have him popping up at all hours of the day and night,' Robert said. The Whitings' house is, of course, on the campus.

Later Robert said to me that he'd mentioned the matter to his 'old man' who said that he didn't care who dug the hole as long as it wasn't him!

Wednesday 5.9.90

Back to school, tra-la tra-la. My last year in the old place and, of course, this is the last year that the old place will *be* the old place. The builders are still making deliveries – no one's started *building* anything yet – but there were stern warnings issued over the Tannoy about falling into holes, cement mixers and so on. The real trouble will blow up when the builders finally arrive and start harassing the girls. I can't imagine this building site will be any different from any other building site and we all know what builders are like, don't we? Phwooooarrrr, get 'em out for the lads, etc. If they try it on some of our ladies they could be in for a shock.

Several people remarked on the Voyage of The Feelie, mainly to the effect that the rose bed looked better without it, which is undeniable. By the end of the afternoon The Feelie had acquired a brand new traffic cone. The supply of traffic cones will be plentiful as they have sprouted thickly on either side of the main entrance, to restrict parking so that the builders' lorries can turn without causing mayhem. I noticed that the lamp standard at the corner is already leaning at an angle of 45°.

Although, as I said, The Feelie was mentioned, no one said anything about Time Capsules. Clearly no one else on Gerry's committee confided anything to their little brothers and sisters. Trust Gerald to form a committee. I wonder who else was on it. Quite a lot of people now in the school may have had elder siblings (useful word) who put things in that capsule, but presumably nobody thinks it's any big deal. Or else they've all left town.

They've almost certainly left town – except for Young Whiting and Jason. Most people get out of Calderley at high speed.

One shock; Mr Ingle, our history teacher, died during the holidays in a climbing accident. Dan says it was in the local paper, but it's such a rag I never read it. I didn't like him all that much but he was a good teacher and anyway, I'm sorry he's dead. He had a wife and two little kids. If I were married with children I don't think I'd put my life at risk on purpose. I mean, you're at risk every time you step out of the front door, but climbing mountains is asking for trouble. I can't, myself, even see the attraction of dangerous sports. In fact I can't, myself, see the attraction of doing anything that causes pain and discomfort. When I see joggers heaving themselves round the back lanes, flopping and wheezing, I want to say to them, 'I can get like that just by lying in bed, mate.' I enjoy sport, probably because when I was little I could hardly do anything, but I don't pursue it past the point where it stops being enjoyable.

Anyway, we have a new history teacher. *I* have a new history teacher, a Miss L. Ashton. We have not met. The trouble with this school is that you can't get all 580 of us into one room at once, except for the sports hall. I really used to enjoy the first day of term at primary school, especially the autumn, because you could size up all the new teachers. Miss Ashton and I are not scheduled to meet until tomorrow afternoon.

There were pictures on the News of the refugee camps in Jordan. It looks like a full-scale catastrophe already, and war hasn't even broken out yet.

Ironic note. I've lost my door key ... somewhere. *Wouldn't* it be a larf if I'd dropped it in the capsule pit and buried it?

APRIL 22ND 1982 THURSDAY

There has been an argument in the House of Commons over war breaking out while peace talks are going on. The Foreign Secretary says that we may have to fight first and talk afterwards. Meanwhile, the Commander of the Task Force says he aims to impose an air as well as a sea blockade, with Harriers (vertical take-off and landing aircraft) in addition to the nuclear submarines. His warning to the Argentinians was as follows: 'Don't take us on because you will lose.' Odds on the Navy – our Navy – winning are 20-1. I don't know who worked this out. Can people possibly be betting on it as they do on horses or the Booker Prize (a prestigious literary award)?

At last something pleasant has happened. (How strange it seems to look at what I've just written. Have I really been feeling so unhappy?) Cycling to school this morning I overtook Jo-Ann, on foot. She really seemed quite pleased to see me so I stopped and walked with her. I said, 'You look remarkably cheerful,' and she said, 'I am cheerful.' And then she said, 'I thought I was pregnant and I'm not.' I did not reveal that I knew anything about this, of course, but she said, 'I expect you guessed after that day in the library. Everyone knows why girls go into dark corners to cry.'

I told her how pleased I was and then I said, without thinking, 'Who was it?'

She wasn't offended. She said, 'I thought it was Mark Lovell – no, that makes me sound like a slag. I *knew* it was Mark, only it was a false alarm.'

'That'll be nice for Mark,' I said. 'Does he know?' I didn't realize how devious I could be.

'He doesn't know it was a false alarm,' she said. 'And I can't tell him. I suppose you don't know where he is?'

It seems that Jo-Ann told her mother, and mother told father, which would account for father attacking Mark outside Laura Ashley. What happened after that though was rather shocking. Mark disappeared. He actually ran away. Jo-Ann said she didn't know whether it was because of her father or because he couldn't face up to what had happened – what he thought had happened.

'It's not as if I hold him responsible,' she said. 'It takes two to make a baby. But I did want to talk it over with him. Dad was furious because they really couldn't afford to let me stay on for A-levels and he thought it was all going to be wasted. I know my dad's a bit of an animal,' she said, 'but he's never hurt any of *us*. He wants me to get on.'

I think she's too forgiving. I can understand Mark being scared of Mr Rugg, but to run off and abandon his girlfriend when she needed him most strikes me as unforgivable. From what I remember, he wasn't much help to her while he was still here, and apparently he hasn't been in touch since he left which is getting on for three weeks ago. Questions are being asked at school. Jo-Ann says she doesn't know how to get hold of him without telling his parents what happened. Presumably he's keeping in touch and has told them some credible tale or they would have had the police looking for him. Still, he's old enough to leave home if he wants.

I've always liked Mark. I wonder what I would have done in his situation.

The Israelis are bombing Lebanon. I have begun to rethink my plans about the kibbutz.

Thursday 6.9.90

Sir Len Hutton has died.

Parliament is *finally* in emergency debate. Apparently the last time they came back early from holiday – sorry, *recess* – was after the Falkland Islands were invaded. I don't think everyone is so keen to go to war this time. I guess they thought they could handle the South Atlantic because it is sea, and in a way it is *our* sea – unlike the Pacific, for instance. The Arabian deserts are alien. On the News the pictures could be of Mars. I know we've been having hot summers lately, but nothing could have prepared our troops and the Americans for what it must be like out there. I remember a film once where a bunch of astronauts were supposed to be on Mars when in fact the whole thing was being faked in a television studio – *Capricorn One* I think it was called.

I wonder why we do trust photography so much. You still hear people say 'The camera cannot lie', which may be true, but a camera can be pretty confusing even when it's telling the truth, and doctoring photographs seems to be a doddle. I love those old shots of Soviet politicians where someone who was standing next to Stalin fell out of favour and was removed, leaving only his boots or his hat.

For all we know, *everything* we see on television news might have been faked, in a studio. If you don't know anyone who was there, how can you prove whether it happened or not, like the Poll Tax riots in London. How many people bother to *check up* on whether a report is even accurate? It's rather like George Orwell's *Nineteen Eighty-Four* where all the media was controlled by the Government and everything that people were told was fictitious. Like: 'Oceania was at war with Eurasia and in alliance with Eastasia . . . Actually, as Winston well knew, it was only four years since Oceania had been at war with Eastasia and in alliance with Eurasia . . . Officially the change of partners had never happened. Oceania was at war with Eurasia: therefore Oceania had always been at war with Eurasia. The enemy of the moment always represented absolute evil . . . '

I just copied that out, in case you think I'd memorized it. I have now.

If we go to war with Iraq, shall we suddenly be an ally of Iran? And shall we start thinking we've always been an ally of Iran?

If you watch the News carefully you can see the facts change before your very eyes. I don't really remember the sinking of the Argentinian cruiser *Belgrano*, but reading it up recently I've discovered that the first reports, on the 3rd May 1982, said that we sank it while it was inside the 200 mile Exclusion Zone. Then its position 'moved' to the edge of the Exclusion Zone, then just outside it. In the end it turned out that the *General Belgrano* had been sunk by a British sub more than *30 miles outside* the Exclusion Zone and heading for Argentina.

I sometimes think I may be too sceptical to be studying history, but on the other hand, perhaps a good historian ought to be sceptical. Miss Ashton, the new history teacher, seems promising. Ingle will be a hard act to follow but she sounds as if she knows what she is talking about, unlike Willows (economics). She looks very young, though. Someone said she used to go to this school. I think that's perverted myself, spending five years here being educated *and then coming back*. It's bad enough that some teachers leave school, go to college and then go straight back into school again without ever meeting any real people, but to go back to the *same* school . . . I think I'd feel as if I were eating my own tail, like the Ourobouros.

I'm writing this in the sixth-form common room in a free period, and I've just noticed that from the sixth-form common room window now *we* can see The Feelie. God, it's horrible. At 4.30 I'm going down to town to meet Evelyn. It's been five weeks! If it hadn't been for this diary to talk to I don't know how I'd have held out. Just because I didn't mention her much, don't imagine I wasn't thinking of her all the time, gentle reader. Actually, gentle reader, *you* are the problem. If I didn't have this feeling that someone would read this one day, I'd be a lot more revealing, I'm sure. Anyway, I shan't have so much time for it in future, but I don't want to abandon it. Even if it goes right down to a few lines a day during this A-level year, at least I ought to keep it going so that I can take it up again when time permits. It would be terrible to miss out on something, after getting this far. Who knows, it might become a chronicle of the 1990s.

I don't think.

APRIL 23RD 1982 FRIDAY

My father was out last night and again this evening. I remarked, riskily I suppose, upon his absence, at dinner. My mother said there are problems at work.

On the face of it there is nothing strange about this. My father is often out in the evenings but this is always known well in advance and meals arranged accordingly. We keep an appointments calendar in the kitchen for this purpose. Though now I come to think about it there have been several occasions during the last few months, and particularly during the last three weeks, when he has been unexpectedly absent during the evening. No one seems to have remarked on it at the time but it certainly is a break with tradition. I don't know what to think. Actually, what I keep thinking of is Jo-Ann asking us to conceal from her parents that she was seeing Mark Lovell. It's very hard to imagine one's own father in a similar situation.

Mark still has not returned to school but there have been some unexpected developments on that front. Apparently Lucy Ashton has had a letter from him. She mentioned this in our committee meeting at lunchtime. According to Lucy, or according to Mark in the letter he wrote, he was staying with friends for a few days at the end of the holidays and came down with a virus infection. How convenient these virus infections are. I seem to remember he had a virus infection on Saturday April 3rd in which case he must have developed another one shortly afterwards. Jo-Ann and I looked at each other when this came out. She just smiled and said to Lucy, 'Poor old Mark. Let's have his address, Luce, and I'll send him a get-well card.'

Afterwards I said to Jo-Ann, 'Why's he writing to Lucy?' She said she thought they'd always been friends. She also said she thought that Lucy probably didn't know that there had been anything between him and Jo-Ann.

'Well, there wasn't,' she said. 'Only the once.'

I asked her what she was going to do.

'Write and tell him it's safe to come home,' she said.

'What about Lucy?'

'There's no need for her to know,' Jo-Ann said. 'Anyway, she's welcome to him.'

Be that as it may, I feel that Jo-Ann has a very generous nature. On the other hand, it might be as well if Lucy knew what disloyalty Mark is capable of. I really am shocked by what he did and what he left Jo-Ann to face.

I shan't be writing any anonymous letters, though.

In the South Atlantic the Task Force nears its objective. Crews are at defence stations, which seems to be one step down from action stations. They have been issued with 'once only' survival suits, which are intended to keep a man alive for several hours in icy water, instead of several minutes. An uninjured man, I suppose that is.

Friday 7.9.90

I can't bear to watch the News. The people coming back from Iraq, weeping. Relatives weeping. We shouldn't be *allowed* to see this.

And more refugee camps. People living in filth and squalor, dying in filth and squalor. Our people are coming back. The men – sorry, men*folk* – are staying, but at least they aren't dying of starvation.

I mentioned the refugees to someone at school today. She said, 'Oh, I know, it's terrible. But it is *different* for them; they're used to it.'

I suppose she meant, because the refugees aren't Europeans it doesn't matter. Because so many people in Asia live at subsistence level, all Asians can take starvation as a matter of course. I read somewhere that a disaster is only a disaster if it happens close by. The further away it takes place, the less we feel involved.

As though, if you don't *know* the victims you don't feel anything for them except, perhaps, Oh, it's terrible. Take air crashes, for instance. 'No Britons involved,' they say on the News. I always thought that was so people realized that they didn't have to worry about relatives, but you can take it another way: 'No Britons involved so it doesn't affect us. Thank you and good night.' And me, I don't take half as much notice of the foreign news pages in the paper because I can't help feeling, These people have nothing to do with me, when I ought to feel sympathy with *anyone* human. John Donne wrote, 'Any man's death diminishes me because I am involved in mankind.' But it was easier for him, in the seventeenth century; there was so much less of mankind for him to be involved with. I don't think our brains have evolved to keep pace with the size of the world or our knowledge of it. In the Middle Ages you scarcely knew what was going on in the next village. Neanderthal man didn't worry about the human condition – he probably only knew a couple of dozen people. *They* were mankind as far as he was concerned. Our brains aren't big enough to take in all we're supposed to know, these days. As soon as a new disaster happens we forget the last one – we *have* to. I remember 1987, the *Herald of Free Enterprise* – that Channel ferry that sank off Zeebrugge, and drowned hundreds, the Hungerford Massacre when a man just went out one day and shot sixteen people, the hurricane that almost flattened Southern Britain, the Remembrance Day massacre at Enniskillen, the fire at Kings Cross Underground Station – one terrible thing after another. You couldn't take it all in without making room by forgetting something else.

And yet, one morning that same year, in May I think it was, we went down to London by coach, on a school trip, and just as we were slowing down at the traffic lights by Hillingdon station, I looked out of the window and saw a dead fox lying on the verge. It didn't look injured but it was obviously dead; a car must have struck it. I was upset seeing that, but glad that someone had laid out the fox respectfully and not left it to get crushed. No one else on the coach had noticed and I didn't say anything, but when we came back that evening I looked out for the fox and saw that somebody else had taken it and laid it among the long grass under the hedge.

Now, a week later, I went up to town again, on the coach, with a friend. We were going to an exhibition,

I think. Anyway, when we got to Hillingdon I looked out specially and under the hedge I could see that the fox was still lying there. I could just see his fur.

After that, all through the year, every time we went up to London I looked out for the fox at Hillingdon traffic lights. One day I saw that the grass under the hedge had been cut, but someone had laid a black plastic bag over the fox. In the end I expect he just rotted down, as if he had been in a wood or a meadow, just how it should have been, and you couldn't see him any more. But I still looked out, each time. I still remembered him. I still do. That was a terrible year, 1987; so many people died, but the only death that stayed in my mind was the Hillingdon fox.

Bob Geldof called it compassion fatigue. I think he was doing himself an injustice. We aren't *meant* to feel so much.

I've just looked up that thing about disasters getting worse as they get closer. It's an equation: '10,000 deaths in Nepal = 100 deaths in Wales = 10 deaths in local town = 1 death next door.'

Q E D.

APRIL 24TH 1982 SATURDAY

I went to the cinema this evening with Will Sargent and Jon Lo. On the way home I said I had to make a phone call and the others went on ahead and I went into a kiosk by the entrance to the covered market. I don't know why I am recording all these details. Shame I suppose. Trying to distance myself from what I did.

I dialled the Patersons' number. I wrote it down before we went out.

Barbara answered. 'This is Barb'wa Paterson speaking.'

I said, 'Is that the Samaritans?'

She said, 'I'm sowwy. This is a pwivate number.'

It was her, all right. The one who rang us, I mean.

I feel horrible doing this.

What's he playing at? Barbara and Mum have been friends since they were at school. How *can* he? How can *she?*

It is believed that the Government has set a deadline for Monday. If by then diplomacy has failed it will use military force. Our destroyers are now in position off South Georgia.

Saturday 8.9.90

Just at the beginning of the News last night I caught something about the Birmingham Six – about unsafe convictions. I was just going out to meet Evelyn so I didn't stay to hear any more. Even so, it doesn't bear thinking about. *Those guys have been in prison almost all my life.* What they were supposed to have done was atrocious; they deserved to go to prison for life, if anybody does. But – suppose they didn't do it? To be honest, I think about them often, more than I do about the Gulf. But not for long. There is so much else to think about. Not for as long as I thought about the fox that died at Hillingdon.

Put in my stint at Chandler's today. I kind of miss it. I asked the roses, 'Have you missed me?' They said, 'Yes, sure, great to see you again.'

Met Evelyn after work. Her parents have persuaded her that she needs to stay in tomorrow and gather her strength for school on Monday. It's just as well, really. True love is a sore distraction and I've got a hell of a lot of work to do.

I was going to tell her about The Feelie and the Time Capsule, but decided that on balance a promise is a promise even if made to a prat like Gerry who is now swanning around LA presumably. Feel that Eve and I should have no secrets from each other, but the capsule isn't my secret.

We have lots of other things to talk about.

APRIL 25TH 1982 SUNDAY

The Argentine Foreign Minister says we are now at war. We have landed on South Georgia. This evening the Prime Minister appeared on the steps of 10 Downing Street and told us all to rejoice.

I am a great admirer of Mrs Thatcher and all that she is doing for this country, unlike many people, and over the matter of the Falklands I think she was absolutely right to meet force with force, but we've only landed on South Georgia; there must be more fighting to come. It seems a little premature to start rejoicing. People are going to get killed.

Geoffrey is spending the weekend with friends near Aylesbury. Hugh was meant to be going as well but he collapsed on Saturday night with a particularly severe attack. My mother was distraught. She has nursed him through so many attacks but they still upset her. I ask myself, just what is my father planning to do with Barbara Paterson? Leave us all? That won't affect me very much as I shall soon be leaving myself, anyway, but the children will be upset.

I'm afraid I don't devote a great deal of space to my little brothers. Please don't think I don't care about them. I do. I just don't find them very interesting at the moment. I hear my mother sometimes on the phone to friends, repeating things that Hugh or Geoffrey has said, remarks that I find neither intelligent nor amusing. But they are nice little boys and I am fond of them, and we are all concerned about Hugh's asthma.

I take it that my father is concerned about Hugh's asthma.

Sunday 9.9.90

President Bush and Mikhail Gorbachev have agreed on united pressure on Iraq. I'm not quite sure what they have in mind as Bush still doesn't rule out force and Gorbachev is keeping quiet on that one.

The Kuwaiti ruling family in exile want force at any price. At anybody's price. They maintain that all Kuwaitis still in Kuwait are being held hostage.

This could turn out to be the War Diaries of Hugh John Marshall. I must get hold of somebody else's war diary and see how they are managed. Things must always have been much the same, for example:

13.10.66 Got up. Milked cow. Dug ditch. Paid tax. Bloody Saxons. Killed boar. Beat wife. Went to bed.

14.10.66 Got up. Milked cow. William the Bastard invaded. Bloody Normans. Spread muck. Went to bed.

The War Diary of Sceorf the Serf.

Phone.

Everybody out but me so I went to answer it.

'Good evening. Could I speak to Gerry Marshall, please?'

'I'm sorry, Gerry doesn't live here any more. He's working in Geneva now.'

'Oh. Could I have his number, please?'

'Yes, but he's in the United States at the moment.'

I gave his number in Geneva.

'If he gets in touch could you say that Mark Lovell called. You won't remember me, I expect. I'm an old friend of his.'

Now, I don't precisely remember him, but could this be the Mark Lovell who is such a pain in the neck on

behalf of the Calderley Conservative Association?
Keeps popping up on telly at Party conferences.

APRIL 26TH 1982 MONDAY

Now, at last, we are calling the conflict a war. Could this be anything to do with the fact that we have recaptured South Georgia? I am beginning to be reminded of the First World War when thousands of men could die fighting to recapture a wood. Of course, on South Georgia, thousands of men have not died, but as far as I can remember there was nothing on South Georgia in the first place, except an old whaling station. Perhaps it is of strategic importance.

My father has announced that he is going away next weekend. He says he is going to attend a management conference in Eastbourne. My mother said, 'That's a bit sudden, isn't it?'

My father said, 'I wasn't going to bother but the original keynote speaker has had to cancel and his substitute is going to be worth hearing.'

My mother said, 'But we're taking the boys to the theatre on Saturday night.'

My father said, 'Oh damn, sorry, darling. Perhaps Gerry can use my ticket?'

My mother said, 'I don't see why Gerry should give up his evening. It's hardly his kind of play. I'll ask Barbara if she'd like to go.'

I was in the hall while all this took place in the kitchen, so I couldn't see anyone. I can't even imagine how my father looked.

He said, '*Barbara?* But we haven't seen them for ages.'

My mother said, 'No, *we* haven't seen *them*, but *I* see *her*. I'll give her a ring, later. I do wish you wouldn't spring these things on me, Tony.'

She very rarely speaks sharply to my father, but even so, I think she was simply annoyed at having the boys' theatre treat disrupted. For a moment, when she said 'Barbara' I thought, she knows. She's testing him. But now I don't think that at all. I don't know what to think, but I am sure she is entirely innocent. And I may be entirely wrong about everything.

The Capsule Committee has now called a halt to contributions unless something utterly fascinating turns up. So many of the contributions are so far short of fascinating and we have already more than will fit into the capsule. Naseem and Robert spent the lunch hour trying to fit in all the things that we really want to include, like William's video and the collection of ephemera. I gave a showing of the video to the committee, operating it myself and starting well after the incriminating part. As William is not on the committee he was not there to observe what I was doing and no one seemed to notice that it was rather short.

'Don't forget to leave room for Gerry's diary,' Lucy said. Naseem looked at me, then. There is something else that I must leave room for.

Monday 10.9.90

Peculiar conversation with Miss Ashton this morning, after class.

Miss A: I've just realized, you must be Gerry's brother. You're not much like him, are you? [An indisputable fact.]

Self: You just missed Geoff. We were both here last year.

Miss A: I was at school with Gerry. I don't suppose you remember me; Lucy Ashton.

Self: Actually, no.

Miss A (*With a light laugh*): I must have changed a lot. You certainly have.

Self: I don't really remember any of Gerry's friends. We were usually out or in bed when they came round.

Miss A: Whatever's happened to Thrust 15?

Self: Well, they've moved it, haven't they?

Miss A (*Peering through the window at said Feelie*): I can see that. It was rather a shock. When I came up for the interview it was still where I remember it.

Self: When was that?

Miss A: The end of August. It was very rushed . . . you know, Mr er, my predecessor . . . they'd had to advertise in a hurry.

Self: You just missed it. It went on the 31st. [I suddenly began to guess what was coming. And it came.]

Miss A: I was there when it was erected. We buried a Time Capsule under it.

Self (*Indecent haste*): I don't know anything about that. Gerry didn't talk to us much in those days . . . we were so much younger . . . we still are.

Miss: It must still be there.

Self: Mmmm. It'll *really* be buried now, won't it? Under the new wing.

Miss A: I suppose so. (*Squints out of window at building site.*) It's hard to tell exactly where it was, isn't it?

That is certainly the case. Since The Feelie took up its bed and walked the quadrangle has started to look like the Ypres Salient. Trenches, mud, the remains of trees, caterpillar treads, water. The Feelie pit, which was a fairly distinctive blot on the landscape, is now just one more blot. I filled it in, of course, very roughly, and now the bulldozers have been over it a few times you can't see where it was.

She went off to her next lesson then. It was only after she'd gone I realized what I'd let myself in for. As matters stand at the moment Miss Ashton thinks the Time Capsule is still where they put it in 1982. On the other hand, the Whitings know that I dug it up. It's not exactly a secret any more, since Bob told Jason.

Problem 1. It is meant to be a secret.

Problem 2. Miss A. is bound to find out that I lied to her and wonder why. Oh dear.

Problem 3. I *think* I asked Jason not to talk but I'm not sure.

Oh *dear*.

APRIL 27TH 1982 TUESDAY

The nation is feeling very cheerful about the recapture of South Georgia. Some kind of landing on the Falkland Islands themselves is likely during the next few days, before the weather closes in. It is winter in the South Atlantic. There is very little time now left for a peaceful settlement. Nine hundred paratroopers have joined the Task Force.

Mark has returned to school. I realize now that of all his friends only Jo-Ann and I know that there was anything suspicious about his absence. Everyone else took his excuse, that he had been ill, at face value. At break Will Thomson said to me, 'Now we've got the whole Upper Sixth together let's get a photo taken. It may never happen again.'

It seemed that he'd been waiting for Mark to come back and praying that no one else would drop out. He did photography at O-level and had arranged with Mrs Huxford, who teaches it, to act as photographer and 'capture' us all for the Time Capsule. We all posed at the end of the afternoon. Will is going to see to the developing and enlargement. We shall sign the back of it.

But it did make me aware that time is running out. One week from tomorrow the sculpture, Thrust 15, will be erected, which means that the capsule will have to be buried on Tuesday. I shall seal it the night before, so we shall be parting company, you and I, on Monday May 3rd. I have rung Jason and asked if he can dig the hole this coming Sunday.

'I thought you'd never ask,' he said.

When I came home from school I asked my mother if she'd yet rung Barbara Paterson about going to the theatre on Saturday. She said, 'Yes, but she's going to be away as well. *Do* you want to come with us, Gerry? Don't feel you have to say yes, but it would be nice not to waste the ticket.'

I said, 'You could give it to a starving student at the door,' but she said she didn't think it was the kind of play to attract a starving student.

I said I'd go with them. That I'd like to. This isn't true. I don't enjoy going to the theatre at all, especially with children, but it is the least I can do.

Everything seems so obvious to me and yet my mother suspects nothing, I swear. Why should she? When you trust people you *don't* suspect them. She thinks she has no reason to distrust my father and Barbara Paterson, her husband and her oldest friend, the people she has most reason to trust. And me, of course.

Tuesday 11.9.90

Three thirty: a dirty great BMW roars up the front drive, scattering builders and goes into a four wheel drift round the rose bed. Merchant banker type leaps out and stands looking at The Feelie. Is too far away for me to make out his _exact_ expression, but can see from the way he is standing that he is surprised. Assume at first that he is simply surprised to see it at all. It's not quite what one would expect to find in the middle of a bed of roses.

Then who should come tripping out but our Miss Ashton. Merchant Banker delivers chaste peck on cheek. Muted roar from passing Third Years. Brief conference follows, evidently on the subject of The Feelie. Both parties climb into car and zoom off.

Voice behind me (Dan Campion) says, 'Some people have gone up in the world.'

'Who?' says I.

'The Yuppie,' says Dan. 'William Sargent, late of this dump. My sister used to go out with him. Then he went into the City and redesigned his lifestyle. Guess who got redesigned out?'

Dan's sister Justine is a medical student. Brilliant. Beautiful. But not brilliant and beautiful enough, apparently for a social-climbing, BMW-owning git like W. Sargent who, said Dan, wrote and told her he felt they were growing apart, just when she was thinking they were growing together.

On the way home it occurred to me that if a fabulously clever and lovely woman like Justine Campion isn't good enough for him, what's he doing with a nice, rather ordinary-looking school teacher like Miss Ashton?

Can I be alone in finding it more than a tad suspicious that suddenly, just as I dig up the Time Capsule, who should come out of the woodwork but all these old school chums? To date, Ashton, Sargent, Ames, Whiting, and Lovell.

Probably I am alone. I'm the only one who *would* find it suspicious. I wish Gerry would ring. Gone to ground in LA. Could he be on the lam?

Chill out, Marshall. Whiting was already on the spot and so was Jason Ames. Miss Ashton *has* to be a coincidence. It's not as if she arranged for Ingle to fall off his Dolomite.

Lovell and Sargent are another matter.

I see I didn't even give the Gulf a mention yesterday. It looks as if a deal with Iran is on the cards. Think of it – Iran and the UK on the same side. Moscow and Washington on the same side. It *is* like *Nineteen Eighty-Four*. I read recently that many Americans don't believe that the USSR was on their side during WWII. In forty years' time, I wouldn't mind betting, most Americans won't believe that the USSR ever *wasn't* on their side. Iran must have trouble remembering whose side it's on.

Sooner or later someone is going to tell Miss Ashton that I dug up the Time Capsule. Mr Whiting could have mentioned it to *anyone*.

APRILE 28TH 1982 WEDNESDAY

Argentina has rejected further peace proposals from Haig and expects Britain to attack the Falklands within forty-eight hours. The public here seems to expect it too, and expects to win. I don't think that there is very much doubt that we shall, but it certainly won't be a 'piece of cake'.

It's easy to want a war that's going to happen 7,000 miles away. We don't face aerial bombardment, blockades, rationing, an army of occupation.

My father says he will be away until next Monday night. I looked in his desk diary this evening. There is nothing written in for the weekend. I know he said that this conference was a last-minute thing, but I would have thought by now he would have noted down hotel details and so on. And there is a line drawn through Monday, which is the May Bank Holiday. He was going to keep it free for something. Us, perhaps. Whatever it was has gone by the board.

Hugh is ill again.

I wonder if Dad will go to Eastbourne, or wherever he is going, if Hugh is ill at the weekend.

Wednesday 12.9.90

We are going to send troops and tanks to the Gulf. The Challenger tank is expected to perform well in desert conditions. It ought to. It was developed for sale to Iran, back in the days when we were selling them things. I expect we'll be selling them things again, soon. Any day now.

I was watching a spy film on telly last night, *The Fourth Protocol*, a quaint tale of the old Cold War. In it someone mentioned Afghanistan. Whatever became of Afghanistan? One more horror story we don't have room to remember, like Lockerbie. The Department of Transport has just published its official report on the airliner that blew up over Lockerbie at Christmas, the year before last. I don't think I've even mentioned it in this diary. 259 people died. The other day I wrote about the sinking of the cross-Channel ferry, the *Herald of Free Enterprise*. Today the trial started of those held responsible. Did they ever hold a trial for those responsible for the *Titanic*?

Did they ever decide who was responsible?

Perhaps it requires large numbers of people to die before anyone bothers to investigate (the *Titanic* would certainly qualify). These things cost time and money, you know. A few years ago there was a spate of attacks on Asian shopkeepers in the town. One man was stabbed to death, Farid Amin. I remembered that because his cousin was in my form the year I went to the comprehensive, and *he* had only left the year before.

This guy was home on vacation from Cambridge and his family said he had been fighting off a man who attacked his father in their shop. Witnesses said he started the fight. The police said there was no racial motive. The Asian community held a silent vigil during the inquest. No one took much notice, but people at school said that Farid would never start a fight.

APRIL 29TH 1982 THURSDAY

I went into town at lunchtime. I ought to have been with the Capsule Committee who now spend all their spare time putting things into the capsule and taking them out again. They remind me of Eeyore with his honey pot and the burst balloon.*

I was actually on an errand for Mr Willows but I wasn't sorry to get away. Then I was sorry I had got away. After I had collected the files for Willows I went into the Chiltern Centre to get a coffee and a sandwich. There is a take-away snack bar on ground level, and overlooking it is a restaurant cum wine bar with an open balcony on the upper level. As I was waiting in the queue my mother and Barbara Paterson came out onto the balcony with a tray and sat down together. My mother saw me and waved. They both waved.

What am I going to *do*? I can't go up to my father and say, 'I believe you are having an affair with Barbara Paterson, please stop.' I still feel there's a chance I might be wrong and even if I weren't, he could easily deny everything. I don't have any proof.

I'm sure the only reason I've become so suspicious is that I'm writing everything down. It's in black and white. I can't blame a faulty memory. I wish I'd never started this diary. It was never meant to be personal at all, simply a day-to-day account of what was happening in the world and here in Calderley. I only put us in to make it more interesting. I should have given the job to someone who can write. I don't have any style. I can't make things interesting. I don't even enjoy writing, not in the way Will Thomson does, for instance. What I've used this diary for is someone to talk to. I have all these friends but no one to confide in. What I have to decide now is whether or not I'm going to put it in the Time Capsule. If I do I can't possibly let the others see what I've written.

The Argentinians say that the Falklands could be 'Britain's Vietnam'. The Commander of the Task Force predicts a long and bloody campaign. The Americans are talking about a 'last chance for peace' plan. From noon tomorrow (British Summer Time, 11.00 GMT), the Maritime Exclusion Zone will be extended to cover civil and military aircraft, as well as ships.

* From a classic children's book of the 1920s, still popular: *The House at Pooh Corner* by A.A. Milne.

Thursday 13.9.90

Another air fatality. Yesterday a Jaguar from RAF Coltishall crashed into the sea, killing the pilot. Why bother to go to war? We can kill off our armed forces at home.

The United Nations has returned to its old habits and is split on the issue of a food embargo to Iraq.

I read that there is massive support from the electorate for the Government action in using force in the Gulf. If this ever gets read in the future you may be envisaging mass demonstrations in the streets of London, shouting, marching and burning Saddam Hussein in effigy. Don't kid yourselves. This is all down to opinion polls. I was talking to Mum about this. She said that never in her life had she been canvassed by any opinion poll. She is forty-nine. Who do they ask?

Eve says that there was a peace protest in town.

Do you know, I haven't told Evelyn anything about the Time Capsule. I am beginning to feel deeply suspicious about the whole thing. I think I said that before. Well, I'm getting deeper. I'm starting to think now that what I said in the beginning is somewhere near the truth. I was joking about Gerry having buried a corpse. I don't really believe that, but I've begun to get the impression that there is something in that capsule that is worrying people. Otherwise, why is everyone being so *oblique* about it? Sooner or later word is going to get around that not only has the thing resurfaced but that I've got it. Someone's noticed already. Dad came in this evening and said, 'Is that your rubbish in the shed?' Everything of mine is rubbish as far as he is concerned so I didn't take it to heart. I said it was some school stuff I was minding for a friend.

'Well, get it out of the way,' he said.

I shouldn't complain. I think this is the first conversation that we have had for a fortnight. I treasure it.

APRIL 30TH 1982 FRIDAY

I brought the capsule home for the weekend to get it packed. I shall seal it on Monday. The committee finally voted on the contents but I think one or two minor items may have to come out to make room for Naseem's letter in its Jiffy bag and for this diary, if I do decide to put it in. Neither of them takes up much room in itself but the same can be said of everything else. As it is, the lid will scarcely close. What I shall have to do is bind it very tightly with strong packaging tape and then chain it, before I wrap it in the bin liners. The chains may have struck you as excessive when you come to open it, but I don't want to risk the thing bursting open and damp getting in. On Sunday Jason will dig the hole and on Tuesday, before school, we will bury the capsule and fill it in. On Wednesday they will lay the slab over it and erect Thrust 15.

My father was on the phone for a long time this evening. He leaves for Eastbourne first thing in the morning.

We have an extension in the kitchen as well as the main phone in the hall. I have to admit that if it weren't for the give-away background noises when you lift the receiver I would have listened in on some of those conversations tonight. That's what I've come to.

Still, he really is going to Eastbourne. My mother said, 'Don't forget to let me have the number of the conference centre, for emergencies.' She meant Hugh. He said, 'I shan't be at the centre, I didn't book in time. I'm staying in an hotel.' He wrote the number on a pad by the phone, so presumably it's a real hotel and he'll really be staying there under his real name. Who will *she* be, I wonder? Mrs Marshall II? Or will they book in separately? That would be safest.

It is an effort to write about the Falklands, but I undertook to do it so I will bring you up to date. Argentina has established its own 200 mile Exclusion Zone around the islands and its mainland territory. Its military are on 'yellow alert', one degree short of full war footing. It is possible that we will launch an early bombing attack to put Port Stanley (the capital) airfield out of action.

I am still writing all this as though I meant to put the diary in the capsule. I suppose I can't bear the thought of having written so much and then have nobody read it. In a way it's a comfort to think that one day somebody *will* read it, far into the future when it's too late to do any harm. Now I know how Naseem feels.

Friday 14.9.90

It seems that the men and tanks we are sending to the Gulf will be the biggest troop movement since the Falklands. As we haven't been fighting anybody since the Falklands this isn't so very surprising. I don't count Northern Ireland; that is *civil* war, whatever you choose to call it.

I'm writing this in the common room at lunchtime. Do I imagine it or has Miss Ashton been giving me funny looks? The man in the BMW turns out to be 'just an old friend'. The girls had no shame about asking her if he was her fiancé. Tassy said that she'd seen her in town with a cop, but Dan thinks that must have been her brother. But it was the fiancé who drove her to work this morning, in a Ford Sierra. More amazement, this time among the blokes. Apparently he is Mr Chaudhuri, the demon gymnastics coach from Mercery Lane.

Just as long as she doesn't send *him* round to rough me up when she discovers my little white lie . . .

We've been burgled. Daylight robbery, literally, though as far as we can make out, nothing's been nicked except the milk money which Mum left on the hall table. Horrible feeling, though, knowing someone's been through the house, *touching* things, personal things. As the cops pointed out, it could have been a lot worse, knowing what some burglars do to kill time. None of the neighbours saw anything and we were all out, though Mum could have come back from the bureau at any moment.

Funny about the milk money, there are plenty of things in this house worth nicking: video, telly, hi-fi (two), computer, Mum's jewellery, though she doesn't have much. And there wasn't any sign of ransacking; it was mainly cupboards that had been gone through.

Oddest of all, they hadn't broken in. As the last one out of the house this morning (Geoff's in Wales) I got blamed for not shutting the front door properly, or leaving it on the latch. But that ain't the case. I *always* bang the door to make sure. Second nature. And the back door was bolted.

2 am. Woke up suddenly with an idea. Could it have been someone looking for the capsule?

Crazy.

We checked the shed door in case someone had been after the mower but the padlock was on and nothing was touched. Since Dad told me to move it the thing's been in with the peat and fertiliser sacks. It was still there.

5 am. I've just thought – my key.

MAY 1ST 1982 SATURDAY

Morning. My mother has just taken the boys shopping. My father left at eight, in the car. I happen to know that my mother would have liked the car both to shop and to drive up to London to the theatre tonight. He could easily have gone by train. More easily than we can, and more cheaply.

As soon as the house was empty I rang the number my father had left; the Imperial Hotel, they said. I asked if they had a Mr Anthony Marshall staying there? They said yes, but he hadn't checked in yet. I hadn't expected him to, but at least I know where he'll be.

I should have asked if Mr *and Mrs* Marshall would be staying. I was going to.

I didn't have the nerve.

The United States has finally taken our side in the Falklands conflict. They are applying sanctions, suspending military exports and loaning Galaxy transport planes to airlift a back-up squadron of Harriers. We are now enforcing a Total Exclusion Zone.

The capsule is packed. You know what I have put in it. I have not read the 'letters to the future' but I've no doubt a lot of them are as libellous as this diary. Do not imagine that I've written anything untrue, but people will call the truth a libel if they don't like it, and sue, if they think they can get away with it. Simon Ashton might, for example. Still, if what Naseem says is true, then his actions ought to be made public, especially if he becomes a figure of universal respect, such as a Member of Parliament.

And my father deserves it too.

Saturday 15.9.90

Well, do I know the whole truth, or don't I?

This morning, at Chandler's, while I was setting out boxes of spring bulbs, Jason Ames suddenly appeared from behind the fruit trees and I realized he'd been waiting for me. It was all very hole-and-corner, like a rendezvous between spies.

He said, 'Can you talk?'

I said it wasn't a particularly good moment, how about lunchtime?

'Where'd you have lunch?' he said. I said in the coffee shop normally, and he said, 'Would they mind if you brought it out here?' I said they wouldn't so he said he'd be back at twelve and sort of drifted away.

After that I spent the morning looking over my shoulder in case the CIA leapt out of the rhododendrons. I was getting really nervous, as if there was a gun trained on the back of my neck. When it was lunchtime I shoved a burger in the microwave and took it out to the end of the fruit tree section. There's never much trade Saturday lunchtime. It picks up again around two, when people have finished their other shopping, I expect. Jason was already there.

He said, 'Have you had any hassle?'

I told him about the burglary, and the key, and the phone call from Lovell, and all about the way Gerry had been panicking about anyone else getting to the capsule first.

I said, 'I think there's something in it that somebody doesn't want found.'

Jason said, 'I think a lot of people _think_ there's

something in it that they don't want found.'

I told him about my original (joke) suspicion that there might be a body down there with it. He said, 'Well, there can't be a body *in* it unless it went through a car-crusher first. Where's the capsule now?'

I must have hesitated a bit, because he said, 'Oh, come on. I'm not going to bust in after dark and nick it, am I? If I'd wanted it I'd have dug it up long ago. At least I knew *where* to dig. Nobody else did.'

I said, 'Was Gerry on his own then, when it was buried?'

He said, 'Gerry wasn't even there.'

'You mean he didn't bury it himself?'

Jason said, 'I just told you, he wasn't there at all. It was due to go in on the Tuesday morning, before school. I dug the hole on the Sunday and the next day I went round to tell him it was all ready, required depth and so on. He said something had come up and he might not be able to get to school the next day. He asked me if I'd come round in the morning, and if he wasn't there, take the capsule up to the school for him.'

'You mean, *you* buried it?' I said, and he said no, he'd picked it up on the Tuesday and took it to the school at 8.30, when the others had agreed to meet for the interment (his word).

'They were expecting Gerry. You should have seen their faces when *I* rolled up,' he said, 'the celebrated criminal and drug addict.'

'Were you?' I said. It seemed to be no-holds-barred time.

'Oh, give it a rest,' he said. 'I used to smoke grass. I was kicked out of school for persistent disruption and truancy and I had a run-in with the law over some spare parts.'

'Spare parts of what?' I said.

'Motors,' he said, with a patient sigh. 'My uncle's used car business. He was as bent as a nine pound note – still is. I got done for handling but they gave me a conditional discharge. Don't even have a record. Point is,' he said, 'everyone knows. They've mainly got it wrong, but I've nothing to hide. I never was respectable and I'm not now. The other lot, the Capsule Committee, they were respectable, though. They kind of withdrew their skirts when I rolled up with their sodding capsule. Even the blokes. They were all standing there, round the hole I'd dug. Remember, I was used to seeing people standing round holes I'd dug, so I just went straight over, lowered the capsule into the hole and started intoning the burial service . . . "Forasmuch as it hath pleased Almighty God of his great mercy to take unto himself . . . " Didn't go down at all well.'

'Who was there?' I said.

'The committee,' Jason said. 'Bob Whiting, Will Sargent, Naseem Whatsit, another Will, Mark Lovell, another bloke . . . there were about ten of them. They were furious. You could see it on their faces; you know, how dare this creep even touch the *hem* of their capsule. All except Jo-Ann.'

I didn't know any Jo-Ann, I said.

'Jo-Ann Rugg,' he said. 'She was a really nice kid, Jo-Ann. Everybody liked her. She went up to Manchester to study drama. She's Jody Rodgers now. On telly. You know.'

I know. She's an alternative comedian and very funny. I knew she was local, but I didn't know her name was Rugg. The only Ruggs I can think of run a fish shop in Union Street.

'She came over and gave me a kiss,' Jason said. 'She was really sweet, that girl. She deserved to get on. The others didn't, though. Miserable bastards. So I left them to it. I had been going to explain that I'd dug their hole to one side of where the sculpture was going, so that they'd be able to get it out, or their descendants would, because you couldn't tell just by looking, but I took one look at them and thought, sod you, and buggered off. I went back though, that evening, and tidied up the hole so there wouldn't be any problem when they came to lay the slab next day. I'd promised Gerry that. No,' he said, 'they didn't want to speak to me then. But you'd be surprised how many of them want to speak to me now.'

'I wouldn't,' I said, feelingly, 'but why? *Is* there something in it?'

'I don't know,' he said, 'but if there is, your brother must have put it there. It was already sealed up when I collected it. Your mum gave it to me when I went round for it.' He was quiet for a bit, then he said, 'This is all my fault, you know, Hugh. I swear, I don't know what's in it, but I pretended I did. Not at the time, that wouldn't have been fair; it was about four years later. They'd all gone off to poly or uni or wherever. They hardly came near this place. Then I met one of the guys – Tim Finch, he was OK really, but we met in a pub and he was with some friends he didn't want me to meet. That's how it felt, anyway. So I said, "You know what, Tim, I haven't seen you since we buried that Time Capsule," and he said no, that was probably true, and – I couldn't help myself, they all looked so pleased with themselves – I said, "That was a proper little time bomb you buried down there," and I kept hinting at all the shocking revelations that were buried with it.

Trouble is,' he said, 'either there *were* some shocking revelations, or else they've just got very guilty consciences.'

'What the hell could they have done?' I said. 'They were only eighteen.'

'I don't suppose they did much,' Jason said, 'but look at some of them now. In the police force, in politics, on telly, teaching. What's your brother doing, Hugh?'

'Something nuclear,' I said.

'Can you get hold of him? Find out what's really in it?'

'Not at the moment. He's in the States,' I said.

'Well, look after it,' he said. 'Bury it again, if you like. I'll help.'

We talked a bit more and agreed to meet for a drink some time. I like old Jason. I think Gerald must have done, too. Jason didn't have any hard words for *him*.

MAY 2ND 1982 SUNDAY

Yesterday, British jets, led by one of the Vulcans, bombed the runway at Port Stanley airfield. The war has begun.

We went to London by train yesterday. The play was fairly terrible but the children enjoyed it. I think my mother did, too. The children slept all the way home in the train. I do think he might at least have let us use the car. I asked my mother what exactly was the trouble between Chris and Barbara Paterson. First of all she said it was none of my business, but in the end she told me that Chris's job took him away from home for long periods of time and that now Barbara thought he wanted a divorce. That Barbara was very lonely and disheartened and hated her job. And now she thought Chris had found someone else and she felt a failure.

I said, 'Hasn't Barbara found anyone else?' and she said, 'Good God, give her a chance, Gerry. She's not one of your friends, falling in and out of love all the time. She needs to get over all this, first.'

I said, 'You've known her a long time, haven't you?'

She said, 'About thirty years.'

I didn't say any more.

She *doesn't* know.

I've been thinking (I'm writing this at one in the morning). I could leave things as they are.

I don't like my father. I can't remember when I first realized this. It is not like saying 'I hate my father'. We all hate our parents from time to time. I simply do not like him. It took a long time to come to terms with it. I can't even explain properly exactly what it is I do feel.

What it comes down to is that if he were just someone I knew I would avoid his company. I love my mother very much. Perhaps she would be better off without him, if he really can do this to her with her best friend. On the other hand, she would be left to bring up the boys alone. I shan't be here much longer. Would she *want* him to stay if she knew? Does he intend to leave us? Or does he think he might as well go on like this, having the best of both worlds: a comfortable home and a loving wife *and* a bit on the side?

Perhaps he is thinking of ending it all this weekend. I'd almost forgotten that all this came to light because of Barbara's phone calls. She was the one who kept trying to get in touch.

If it *was* her.

I don't even have any proof that she's with him in Eastbourne.

I could find out.

Sunday 16.9.90

Headline in the paper: SCREW TIGHTENS ON SADDAM. I wonder. Will it all blow up next week or will we still be sitting here in six months' time, tightening screws etc., while arms and men and tanks pile up in the Saudi Arabian desert?

It sounds so chatty, calling him Saddam. Not even Mr Hussein. 'I say, Saddam, old chap . . . '

I've been having another look at the capsule. In spite of all the bin liners the chains are rusty. Bolt cutters would easily go through that padlock hasp. I am going to have to open it, whatever Gerry says, because the more I think about it the more certain I am that this is what the burglar was after. Someone found my key and *knew* it was mine. I must have been right when I thought I'd dropped it in the Feelie pit, only I didn't bury it.

There is a guy I never saw before today, who has passed the house three times this morning. Maybe I'm getting paranoid, but

But.

I'll go through the contents and if there's anything really inflammatory I'll *lose* it. If there's anything criminal I don't know what I shall do. Take it out and hide it, I suppose, before anyone else comes round asking heavy questions. With Gerry safely out of the way I can say that perhaps he didn't have room to include − whatever it turns out to be.

I have a feeling though that Jason's theory is the right one − that there's nothing inside but guilty consciences.

MAY 3RD 1982 MONDAY

This is the last entry I shall make in this diary. It has not turned out as I intended, but I can't bring myself to destroy it and I can't bear to keep it. As you know, I am putting it in the capsule.

Jason dropped in this morning to tell me he had dug the hole to the required specifications. I told him that I might not be able to get up to school tomorrow to bury the capsule. Could he possibly take it for me? I would have asked one of the others but Jason was there and wanted to help. And he doesn't ask questions.

He never did write that treatise on twentieth-century burial customs.

It is 10.45 pm. Just now my father rang to say that he would be home late tomorrow evening. My mother took the call. I heard her laugh and say, 'Can't you tear yourself away, then?'

I am going to miss school tomorrow. I shall go to Eastbourne.

If I find them there together I shall say

I do not know whether I am doing this on my mother's behalf or just out of revenge, but whichever it is, it will be a form of blackmail. 'That is a very nasty word' as they say in old films, but I am going to do it. Either they stop seeing each other or I shall tell my mother what is going on. I am sorry things turned out like this.

At 8 o'clock last night one of our nuclear submarines torpedoed an Argentinian warship, inside the 200 mile Exclusion Zone. It was a cruiser, the *General Belgrano*.

83